MEET THE CRAWFORD FAMILY

Joe Crawford: Eldest son and reclusive bachelor.
He believes no woman would have him, but he
craves a family and will enter into a marriage of
convenience if it means finally getting what he
desires.

Anna Pointer: With two children to raise, this
widow couldn't refuse Joe's proposal of marriage.
But her secret desire for her husband could lead to
heartache like she never imagined.

Pete Crawford: The happily married second son
has plenty of advice to give his older brother…
even if Joe doesn't want to hear it.

Carol Crawford: This family matriarch just wants
all of her children to settle down and be happy.
She believes Joe's marriage to Anna will bring him
all the joy he deserves and she'll stop at nothing to
bring the two together.

Caleb Crawford: The head of the Crawford
family is hiding some scandalous secrets from
his own children. Find out what they are, in
Hush, Judy Christenberry's newest novel from
Silhouette Books, available September 2003.

Dear Reader,

The summer after my thirteenth birthday, I read my older sister's dog-eared copy of *Wolf and the Dove* by Kathleen E. Woodiwiss and I was hooked. Thousands of romance novels later—I won't say how many years—I'll gladly confess that I'm a romance freak! That's why I am so delighted to become the associate senior editor for the Silhouette Romance line. My goal, as the new manager of Silhouette's longest-running line, is to bring you brand-new, heartwarming love stories every month. As you read each one, I hope you'll share the magic and experience love as it was meant to be.

For instance, if you love reading about rugged cowboys and the feisty heroines who melt their hearts, be sure not to miss Judy Christenberry's *Beauty & the Beastly Rancher* (#1678), the latest title in her FROM THE CIRCLE K series. And share a laugh with the always-entertaining Terry Essig in *Distracting Dad* (#1679).

In the next THE TEXAS BROTHERHOOD title by Patricia Thayer, *Jared's Texas Homecoming* (#1680), a drifter's life changes for good when he offers to marry his nephew's mother. And a secretary's dream comes true when her boss, who has amnesia, thinks they're married, in Judith McWilliams's *Did You Say...Wife?* (#1681).

Don't miss the savvy nanny who moves in on a single dad, in *Married in a Month* (#1682) by Linda Goodnight, or the doctor who learns his ex's little secret, in *Dad Today, Groom Tomorrow* (#1683) by Holly Jacobs.

Enjoy!

Mavis C. Allen
Associate Senior Editor, Silhouette Romance

Please address questions and book requests to:
Silhouette Reader Service
U.S.: 3010 Walden Ave., P.O. Box 1325, Buffalo, NY 14269
Canadian: P.O. Box 609, Fort Erie, Ont. L2A 5X3

Beauty & the Beastly Rancher

JUDY CHRISTENBERRY

From The Circle K

SILHOUETTE *Romance*®

Published by Silhouette Books

America's Publisher of Contemporary Romance

SILHOUETTE BOOKS

ISBN 0-373-19678-4

BEAUTY & THE BEASTLY RANCHER

Copyright © 2003 by Judy Russell Christenberry

Books by Judy Christenberry

JUDY CHRISTENBERRY

has been writing romances for fifteen years because she loves happy endings as much as her readers do. She's also a bestselling author for Harlequin American Romance, but she has a long love of traditional romances and is delighted to tell a story that brings those elements to the reader. A former high school French teacher, Judy devotes her time to writing. She hopes readers have as much fun reading her stories as she does writing them. She spends her spare time reading, watching her favorite sports teams and keeping track of her two adult daughters.

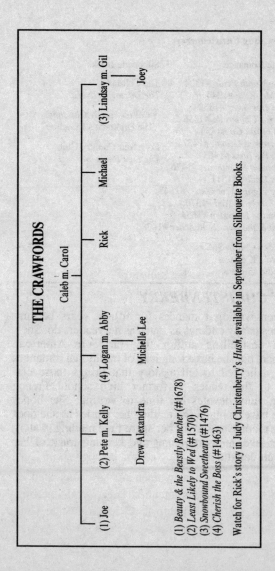

THE CRAWFORDS

Caleb m. Carol

- (1) Joe
- (2) Pete m. Kelly
  - Drew
  - Alexandra
- (4) Logan m. Abby
  - Michelle
  - Lee
- Rick
- Michael
- (3) Lindsay m. Gil
  - Joey

(1) *Beauty & the Beastly Rancher* (#1678)
(2) *Least Likely to Wed* (#1570)
(3) *Snowbound Sweetheart* (#1476)
(4) *Cherish the Boss* (#1463)

Watch for Rick's story in Judy Christenberry's *Hush*, available in September from Silhouette Books.

Chapter One

Joe Crawford shoved back his straw cowboy hat and wiped his forehead with his handkerchief. He'd been on the tractor for more than an hour, plowing the small pasture to prepare it for the alfalfa he intended to plant there.

The field wasn't large, but he hated to let anything go to waste. He could make enough to feed the herd for a month by taking the time to plant this last piece of land he owned. All it would take was a little sweat.

He might not attract the women like his brothers, or produce grandchildren, but he was a hard worker and made plenty of money for his efforts. He'd realized in high school that women weren't interested in him, so he'd turned his attention to studying, earning him a four-year scholarship to Oklahoma State University to study land management. Now, at thirty-five, he figured love had passed him by.

He turned the tractor and started back toward the other end of the field, toward the county road that flanked the land. His gaze drifted to the corner where the road turned south. There was an old fruit stand there, built many years ago. It was on Derek Pointer's old place or Joe would've torn it down. It was an eyesore.

But today it was occupied. Someone had set up shop, selling vegetables and fruit. He couldn't imagine who the widow Pointer had given permission to. Or maybe they were nesters, not asking.

His eyesight was good, so when he caught a glimpse of movement, he looked again and discovered who-ever it was had a potential customer pull to a stop. He noted the two men who got out of a muscle car, not the usual type to be interested in produce.

He shrugged his shoulders. It took all kinds. He shoved the men from his mind. He'd almost reached the opposite end of the field when some movement drew his attention again. This time it was a small child, flying across the barren field between Joe's land and the produce shed.

Joe didn't know how he knew something was wrong, but he did. The child was trying to signal him with her skinny arms. Joe shoved the gear into Neutral and grabbed the hand brake. Then he vaulted from the tractor and met the child more than halfway.

"What's wrong?" he asked.

"Those men are hurting my mommy. Please help her."

He remembered the swagger he'd noticed when the

men got out of the car. He didn't know who was selling the produce, but two against one wasn't fair.

"Stay here. I'll let you know when you can come." Then he raced to the produce stand, his vision blocked by the three-sided structure.

Anguished cries told him the woman was in distress. When he rounded the side of the stand, he saw her, lying on the dirt, one man at her head, holding her hands, and the other on top of her, pulling at her clothes. He didn't recognize either of them. They must have been from out of town.

Joe was a big man, the biggest of the Crawford men. His father had always told him not to take advantage of smaller men. But he knew his father hadn't meant times like this. He swung his mighty fist into the man at her head and he fell back, turning loose of her hands. Then Joe turned to find the other man charging him.

He didn't mind their resistance. It kept them from trying to hurt the woman. He planted his fist in the man's stomach with fierce pleasure. He turned to check on the other man, who had pulled himself together and was coming toward Joe. He never got there.

The woman, Anna Pointer he now realized, had grabbed a board lying on the ground and slung it across the back of the man's head. He silently fell to the ground.

"Nice job," Joe said with a grin, amused by the woman's action. He reached in his pocket for the cell phone he carried and dialed the sheriff's office.

"We've got an attempted rape where Highway 50

turns south, at the old produce stand. Two men attacking a woman. We'll hold them until you can get here.''

He turned back to the woman and discovered her sinking to the ground as if her legs had become too weak to hold her. He reached for her. ''Mrs. Pointer, are you all right?''

He kept some distance between them, letting his arms do all the work. ''Did they hurt you?''

''Just—just bruises. Oh! My little girl—''

''She's okay. What's her name?''

''Julie.''

He found an empty box for her to sit on. He started toward the side of the stand, but a movement and Mrs. Pointer's cry alerted him to the man he'd hit in the stomach. He tried to attack Joe, but the man was six inches shorter and didn't have a lot of muscle.

''No, you don't.'' He hit his jaw hard. Then he picked up a piece of rope lying on the ground. He twisted the man's hands behind his back and tied him up. Then he did the same for the other one.

''Maybe that will hold them for a few minutes,'' he said to the woman and resumed his attempt to bring the little girl to her mother. He expected the child to be where he'd left her, but she'd followed him and stood a few feet from the stand.

''Julie, your mom is fine. She wants to make sure you are, too. Come here.''

Julie came closer, but she skirted around Joe, leaving plenty of distance between them. He wasn't surprised. Children didn't take to him much because of his size and his irregular features. He had dark brown hair with bushy eyebrows and a crooked nose, giving him a gruff look. His four brothers were handsome as sin. Women chased them constantly. Nobody chased Joe. He'd accepted his lot in life, but scaring little children still bothered him.

"Mommy!" Julie cried out as she flew into her mother's arms.

"Oh, baby, I was so worried about you. Are you all right?"

"Yes. Did those bad men hurt you?"

Tears were running down both their faces, and Joe looked away. He felt like he was invading their privacy.

The females were hugging each other when Joe heard a baby cry. He looked around, startled, and found another box serving as a bed for a baby wrapped in a light blanket. The woman went to the box and lifted the baby, bigger than Joe had first thought. He'd forgotten Derek's wife had been pregnant when he'd died in that car crash. It had caused a lot of gossip because he'd had a woman with him, who was not his wife.

"You came here with Julie and your baby? Don't you know how dangerous that can be?"

She lifted her head and glared at him. "I do now."

"You should've figured it out before you put the kids at risk."

"I just wanted to sell my excess produce. Pardon me for not realizing some men would think it a fine opportunity to rape me!"

A siren in the distance stopped Joe from responding. He started to say she should know the nature of men. After all, she'd been married to a man who thought of no one but himself. But he was handsome.

The Sheriff's deputies jumped from the car as soon as it slammed to a stop, sending dirt spraying into the air.

"Crawford, is everything okay?"

"Now it is. These two stopped and, realizing Mrs. Pointer was on her own, had her down on the ground, trying to undress her when I arrived." He looked over at the two men. The one the widow had whacked on the back of the head was just coming to. The other one was sitting up, struggling with the rope.

"I bet they're regretting that decision since you came along," one of the deputies said, grinning at Joe.

"Mrs. Pointer took out the one on the left. He might need some medical attention, though he doesn't deserve it. Neither of them is too bright. And if they show their faces around here again, they won't be leaving."

"You can't prove anything," the one sitting up sneered.

"If you're dead, I won't have to prove anything." Joe's words were softly spoken, hoping Mrs. Pointer wouldn't hear them.

The man turned to the deputies. "Did you hear him threaten me? I'm going to press charges!"

Joe didn't show any fear. Anna Pointer rushed over to his side. "I don't think that will matter once I tell them what you tried to do. Besides, as he said, you come back and you might be dead.''

The two deputies nodded. ''We protect our women-folk around here. And we don't press charges for doing that. You'd better keep your mouth shut. All that would do is confirm that you tried to hurt this lady.''

They pulled both men up and dragged them to the car, putting them into the back seat.

''That rope isn't very strong. You might want to put on handcuffs,'' Joe called.

The deputies did so. One of them called, ''Thanks for reminding us. Sheriff wouldn't be pleased if they got away. Ma'am, we'll call you about pressing charges. Mrs. Pointer, isn't it?''

''Yes. Thank you.''

The men drove off in another cloud of dust, leaving Joe and Mrs. Pointer standing there. She had the baby in her arms with Julie holding on to her shirttail.

''You're not going to do this again, are you?'' he asked, wanting to be sure she understood the danger.

''I won't bring the children back. I'll put them in Mother's Day Out at the church.'' She didn't look at him.

''What? Didn't you understand what was about to happen? What's wrong with you?''

She was a beautiful woman. But her jaw firmed and she looked up at him. ''I won't risk the children, though I need to sell the produce. I've got a bank payment due on the land and I don't have the money for it. I have to sell what I have.''

He stared at her. A wisp of wind would blow her away. Julie, too, looked like she hadn't had a good meal in a while. Only the baby had any fat on him. They weren't starving to death, were they? He looked around at all the produce and fruit she had and told himself he was being ridiculous.

"You can sell at the Farmer's Market in Lawton. You'll make more money there."

"But I would have to pay a fee for the space. Thanks anyway." She began loading boxes into the back of the old rattletrap truck parked beside the stand.

"You quitting for the day?"

"That was the first car to come along in two hours. And I—I don't feel well." She carried more boxes to the truck.

He picked up twice as many as she was carrying and followed her. "Are you sure this thing runs?"

"It did this morning."

He frowned as he loaded his haul. Derek hadn't been a good husband. Joe knew that. He'd heard too much about his social life, leaving his wife at home. But he'd always seemed to have money to spend. Had he left his widow penniless?

"Julie, bring the aprons, please, sweetie," she ordered in a gentle voice.

The little girl picked up the aprons displayed on a piece of rope strung between two poles. Then she carried them toward her mother, dragging them in the dirt.

"Good job, Julie," Joe said and picked her up by the waist, holding her high enough that the aprons didn't get soiled. When he set her down by the truck, she peeked at him from beneath long lashes.

"Thank you. That was fun." Then she handed the aprons to her mother and went back to the baby bed where the baby was fussing.

"She's a good helper," Joe said. She was as pretty as her mother.

"Yes, she is." She cleared her throat. "I don't think I thanked you for your assistance this afternoon."

"I'm glad I was nearby."

They continued to carry her things to the truck until everything was loaded. She politely thanked him again, then she loaded Julie and the baby.

Joe was glad to see a carrier seat in the truck. While she was strapping in her baby, he asked Julie if he could help her with her seat belt.

"I can do it. Mommy taught me."

"You are a smart little girl. I bet your mommy is proud of you."

"Yes. I help her with everything."

"Well, you certainly helped her today."

The woman slipped on her own seat belt and checked Julie to be sure she had hers fastened. "Thank you again, Mr. Crawford."

She cranked the engine. Nothing happened. She pumped the gas pedal and repeated the process. The engine started up, but Joe didn't think it sounded good. It probably needed to be checked out.

She drove away, leaving him standing there, staring after them. Slowly he walked back to his tractor. He didn't have much more plowing to do. In the time it took to finish, his mind was filled with thoughts of the woman he'd just saved. He thought her name was Anna. He hadn't known her husband well because he was about four years younger than Joe. His brothers knew him. They'd talked about what a jerk he was.

It seemed Anna had suffered from her marriage. Not only had her husband betrayed her, but he'd also apparently left her penniless. He looked over the fence at the barren land.

He wondered why she didn't work the land. Or hire someone to do so. Maybe she should rent out the land. That might pay the mortgage. He should ask her.

He shook his head. He knew she wouldn't welcome a visit from him. But he couldn't tolerate their suffering. If he could help her get back on her feet, maybe she'd find someone to marry who could take care of the little family. Someone who'd be good to her and Julie. And the baby. Derek had been a lucky man and he'd thrown it all away.

He finished the plowing and headed for his barn. As soon as he'd put everything in its place, he got in his pickup, a two-year-old model with all the bells and whistles on it, unlike Anna's truck. He was going to find out about Anna Pointer. His mother knew everything going on in the county. She could tell him.

Carol Crawford had just gotten home from her daughter Lindsay's house. She'd spent the afternoon baby-sitting Lindsay's little boy, and her second son Pete's adopted son and newborn baby. She had a smile on her face when Joe joined her in the kitchen.

"Joe! Are you coming to have dinner with us? How nice!"

He gave her a hug and kissed her cheek. "Don't you ever tire of feeding hungry boys?" he asked with a smile. Since she had five sons before she finally gave birth to Lindsay, she'd spent most of her life providing for her growing boys.

"Of course not. How are you? I haven't seen you at all since last Sunday when you had dinner with us."

"I know. I've been plowing the fields. Today I was over by the Pointer place."

"Oh? Did you see Anna? I'm worried about her."

His gaze focused on his mother. "Why?"

"No one ever sees her anymore. She doesn't come to town much at all. And she's got two babies to take care of."

"How old is Julie?"

She was surprised by his question, but he didn't explain.

"I think she's close to four. She was born about ten months after Anna married Derek. Terrible mistake."

"Yeah. Uh, did Derek leave her provided for?"

Carol stopped putting away groceries and turned to face her son. "I assumed he did. I'm sure he had insurance."

"She almost got raped today trying to sell produce at that old stand where 50 turns south."

"What? Oh, no! What happened?"

He gave her a thumbnail sketch of the event. Emphasizing Julie's quick thinking and Anna's determination.

"Well, I certainly hope she learned her lesson!" Carol exclaimed, frowning.

"She said she wouldn't bring the children again, but she had to sell her produce so she could pay the mortgage."

Carol continued to frown as she poured two glasses of lemonade from the refrigerator. "So she doesn't have any income?"

"That would be my guess," Joe said as he held his mother's chair for her and then joined her at the table. "I suggested she sell things at the Farmer's Market in Lawton, but she said she couldn't afford the fee."

"Oh, my. Why didn't she let someone know? The community would have pitched in."

"I'd guess because of her pride. After all, her husband embarrassed her enough." He thought about that stubborn chin she'd shown him.

"Well, we have to do something to help her."

He relaxed a little. He'd known his mother would want to help. "I was thinking of renting some land from her. But I didn't ask her today. I was wondering if you still get free space at the Farmer's Market since you're on the Board of Directors."

"I'd forgotten about that, but yes, I do. Only, it has to be used by me or a family member. I can't give it to Anna, as much as I wish I could."

"If I stayed with her, no one would question her, would they?"

"No, but they might question you about why you're with her. That might prove a little embarrassing for both of you." Carol looked at her son speculatively.

"Come on, Mom, no one would suspect Anna Pointer of having any interest in me. Women don't want someone as ugly as me."

"Joe, I wish you wouldn't talk about yourself that way. You're not ugly!" she protested.

"Of course not!" he replied in a teasing voice. "I just have a face only a mother could love." He'd dealt with the reality of his life in high school. If it was a matter of muscle or brains, they picked him first, but after he'd done whatever they needed, he was abandoned.

"I'd be glad for you to stay with Anna and let her use my space. But you'll have to stay with her. Can you explain it to her, or shall I write a note?"

"I can explain it to her, Mom. And explain that I won't take advantage of her. She might be a little skittish after this afternoon."

"Oh, my, yes."

"I'll go see her after dinner here. You wouldn't have any cookies or something like that to take with me, would you? I think that might take Julie's mind off what happened today. I'd hate for her to have nightmares."

His mother stared at him and his cheeks heated up. "She's just a baby herself, but she saved her mother today."

"True. Why don't I bake a cake? I can do that while you go out and talk to your Dad. He's working in the barn this afternoon. He might be interested in renting some of her land, too. Or he might know others who would be interested."

"Good idea, Mom. That would take care of the mortgage payment. Was she born in the city? Otherwise I'm surprised she isn't working the land herself."

"I don't know, son. Why don't you ask her?"

"I will."

He hurried out to the barn, anxious to tell his father about Anna Pointer. "Dad!" he called as he stepped inside one of the three barns they had.

"Joe? What are you doing here? I thought you were plowing all week," Caleb Crawford called as he came toward his oldest son.

"I am. I ran into a problem today and I wanted to ask your advice."

He told his father about the incident with Anna Pointer. Then he explained Anna's need for money to pay the mortgage.

"I figured Derek had insurance that paid off the land. Hmm, that's difficult, making enough money from produce to satisfy the bank."

"Yeah. I was wondering if you'd be interested in renting some of her land. She's not working it at all. I think she's got a hundred sixty acres in decent shape. I thought I might plant more hay and sell off what I don't need."

"Good thinking. Yeah, I might be interested. However, Pete would probably appreciate knowing about it, too. He's got a family to raise, you know. And his land connects with part of Pointer's, like yours does."

"That's true. Maybe I should go over there after dinner."

"You're going to a lot of trouble for this woman.

Seems to me I remember she's a beauty. You interested in her?''

Joe stiffened. ''You know better than that, Dad. You know I don't attract women like my brothers do.'' He turned away, like he planned on walking out.

''Boy, you make too much of having a handsome face. It's about time you found a woman and settled down. Pete is three years younger than you and he's got two kids. Logan has two kids, too. The other two haven't married yet, but it won't be long. You're falling behind.''

''I'm doing all right. My crops were good last year, and my herd is growing. I've got money in the bank. I'm not complaining,'' he told his father.

''That's just it, son. You need a woman to spend the money you're making. It keeps a man humble and working hard.''

Joe laughed, trying not to sound bitter. ''I can stay humble, Dad. That's not a problem.''

Chapter Two

Anna settled Julie into her bed after reading her one of her favorite storybooks. "All right, sweetie, time to go to sleep."

"Okay, Mommy, but—I want to say thank you to God for the big man. He saved us today."

"Yes, he did. I think that's a nice idea." She listened to her daughter's prayers, hoping Julie wouldn't have nightmares. Then she kissed her good-night.

In the poorly furnished living room, Anna sat down in the second-hand rocker she'd rocked her babies to sleep in. She hoped the rocking would ease her fears. She'd been so stupid five years ago when she'd let Derek talk her into marriage. She realized now that he'd married her because she wouldn't sleep with him. Once he'd had her, he went on to new conquests, ignoring his marriage vows. By then, she was pregnant with Julie. So she told herself he was young and he'd eventually settle down.

But he hadn't. And he'd canceled the insurance she'd thought he had. When he died, she discovered there was no money at all. He'd spent every penny they'd had. Even more. His parents were furious with her. He'd taken money from them and blamed the need on Anna.

After his death, they'd moved to Florida and wanted nothing to do with her or their grandchildren. The land wasn't paid for, there was no money in the bank, and he had no lasting friends. She'd had to sell every piece of machinery on the place to settle his debts.

She'd found it difficult to face the community, embarrassed by her situation. So she'd withdrawn. And hoped she could sell something to pay off the bank.

She'd tilled the garden by hand and raised a good crop. But how was she going to sell them?

She'd tried to brazen her way through Joe Crawford's questioning, but she knew she couldn't go back to today's fiasco.

A knock on her door startled her. She crossed the room in the shadows, grabbing her broom as some form of protection. "Who is it?"

"Joe Crawford."

She didn't want to let him in, but he'd saved her today. She had to at least do that much. "Come in, Mr. Crawford," she said, opening the door.

He stood on her front porch, hat in one hand and a cake container in the other. "I hope I haven't come too late."

"Too late for what?"

"Before Julie's bedtime."

"Come in," she said again. He stepped past her and turned to face her. "I'm afraid Julie just went to bed. You can leave a message for her if you want."

"I'd better leave this instead of a message. My mom baked it. I thought Julie might need something to distract her from what happened today."

His thoughtfulness made her want to cry. But Anna wasn't one of those ladies who melted. It made her angry that he could make her want to weep on his shoulder. Stiffly, she said, "It's very kind of you to think of Julie."

"And you. I don't expect Julie to eat the entire cake." He grinned a little, something he hadn't done much earlier in the day.

She drew a deep breath. "Thank you again."

He stood there awkwardly. It reminded her of her manners. "Would you care to sit down, Mr. Crawford?"

"Yes, I would, Mrs. Pointer."

He continued to stand, looking at her, and she realized he was waiting for her to sit down first. Amazing, Derek's few friends had treated her like a servant.

He sat down, holding his hat between his legs as he rested his elbows on his knees, his gaze lowered. "I need to talk to you."

"Please, Mr. Crawford, don't bring up the subject of my returning to the produce stand. I have no intentions of doing so."

His eyebrows rose. "Glad to hear it."

"Yes, well, it was kind of you to be concerned," she said as she stood. "Thank you again."

He blinked several times. "Is this a bad time?"

"No, of course not, but I thought— Is there something else?"

"Yes, ma'am. I wondered why you're not working the land."

It was her turn to blink. "I—I don't have any tools. I had to sell them. I was embarrassed by Derek's debt and wanted to pay it off as soon as I could."

"Ah. I see. Well, then, would you consider renting the land to me? Not all of it," he hastily added. "My brother Pete would like half of it." He named the going figure for good land.

All Anna could do was stare at him. She'd placed a small ad in the local paper two months ago, but she'd gotten no response. "Why would you be interested, Mr. Crawford?"

"I don't like to see land go to waste. With a little work on my part, I can have a bigger harvest."

"And your brother?"

"He's got two kids to feed. He always needs a bigger crop." Again, he smiled at her.

He looked much friendlier when he smiled. "I—I advertised my land a couple of months ago. No one contacted me." She lifted her chin to challenge him.

"I didn't see it," he said simply.

"I don't want charity!" she snapped.

"Mrs. Pointer, I won't pretend that I need your land to survive, but I can make a profit off it. If you're willing to rent it, why shouldn't I do so?"

"You're sure you want to lease it?" She was trying not to jump from her chair and sing and dance because he'd solved her major problem. "I can make it one way or another if you—" She couldn't really but he wouldn't know that.

"My brother and I are both interested."

"Then, of course, I'd be delighted to rent it to you."

"Great. I'll have my lawyer draw up a lease agreement and bring it by tomorrow. We'd like to split the lease between us. Pete is taking the land that meets with his place and I will use the other side."

"That's satisfactory."

"We'll exclude the acre your house and garden occupy."

"Thank you." She stood again, assuming their business was settled.

"Uh, I have something else to say."

She sank back into the rocker. He was going to lecture her again, which irritated her.

"My mother is on the board of directors of the Lawton Market place. She gets a space free of rent."

Anna had no idea where he was going with this subject.

"I thought you could sell your produce Saturday in town."

"I told you I can't afford—"

"That's just it. I can use the space free. All you need to do is stay with me all day and no one will question you."

"I couldn't do that!"

"Why not?" His voice changed, filled with bitterness. "Why not? Afraid of what people will say?"

She blinked several times, unsure of the reason for his change of voice.

He continued, "I promise I won't take advantage of you."

She turned bright red. "Of course not. I didn't t-think that."

"Good. I'm a confirmed bachelor. I'm not offering because you're pretty, even though you are. And you don't have to pay me back in any form. We're just going to sell some vegetables and fruit. Agreed?"

His words were forceful and she sensed that if she refused, it would hurt his feelings. Besides, his offer was a godsend. First the land and now selling her produce. He was like a genie in a bottle, granting her three wishes.

"Mr. Crawford, I didn't mean—being able to sell my goods there would be wonderful. But it would require you to spend the day in town. I know you have work to do."

"Always," he agreed with another grin, but the bitterness was gone. "I can wait to start plowing your land until Monday."

"You're sure?"

"I'm sure. Will you be here tomorrow?"

"Yes, of course."

"Okay, once the leases are drawn up and I have Pete's check I will come pick you up. Then we'll go to town, take the leases to the lawyer and deposit the money in the bank. We can look at the space we'll have for Saturday. Agreed?"

With her mind whirling, she said, "Yes, that would be wonderful, but—never mind. We'll be ready."

"What is it?"

"I was thinking of my son's nap time, but it doesn't matter."

"Why don't we drop the kids off at my Mom's?" When she started to protest, he held up his hand. "She's already offered. She likes little kids."

"That—that would be wonderful. If something comes up, I can take them with me."

"Fine. I'll tell her you said that. Now, I'll go," he said as he stood, and she was reminded again how tall he was. Julie's prayer for "the big man" was certainly appropriate.

"Mr. Crawford, you've been—so helpful. I can't thank you enough."

"I'm getting more land to work, Mrs—Aw heck, we might as well call each other by our names. Otherwise, no one is going to believe we're friends. I'm happy with our agreement, Anna. I'll see you tomorrow."

"Yes, Joe. Thank you again."

He was out the door before she could reach it and disappeared in the spring night.

Anna awoke the next morning with a spring in her step that had been absent for the last five years. She was going to have enough money in the bank to make the payment and have some left over. If she sold even half her things at the market on Saturday, she could purchase a few things that they needed.

She'd have to be careful though. Another payment would come around sooner than she'd realize. Now, for three whole months, she'd be able to face each day with a smile. She was thrilled. She was also relieved because she'd dealt with pressing charges against the men over the phone last night.

She took extra care with her hair and donned a blue dress that matched her eyes. She didn't bother with makeup. That would be too obvious. When Julie got up, having had a restless night, she did a very un-motherly thing. She fed her cake for breakfast.

"Cake? I get cake?" Julie asked with excitement.

"Just this once. Mr. Crawford brought it over last night especially for you. He was disappointed that you were already asleep."

"He came to see me?" Julie said in reverential tones. Anna realized no one came to see Julie. She had no playmates because Anna kept to herself. She felt doubly guilty at making her daughter pay for her sins.

"Yes, and he's coming back today. He's going to rent our land, honey, and that money will help us out. So everything is going to be better." She lifted Julie in her arms and danced around the table.

"Mommy! I like it when you're happy!" Julie exclaimed with a joyful laugh.

Again Anna felt guilty. She'd been letting their situation drag her down, but she hadn't realized how aware of everything Julie was.

"Everything is going to be better, baby. You'll see."

"Is Mr. Crawford going to stay for lunch?" Julie asked.

"No, we have to do business today. You and Henry are going to stay with his mother while we go into town."

"His mommy? He has a mommy?"

"Why, yes, he has a mommy. Why wouldn't he?"

"'Cause he's so big," Julie said with a look of wonder.

Anna laughed again. "Come to the table, sweetie and start on your cake. I'll pour you a glass of milk."

"Are you going to eat cake, too, Mommy?"

Anna stopped in surprise. With a smile, she said, "You bet I am."

While Pete was signing the lease papers, he said, "If I remember right, Anna Pointer is a good-looking blonde."

Joe grunted and looked at Kelly, Pete's wife.

"How's the store doing?" he asked, deliberately trying to change the topic.

"It's doing great, Joe. Stop by and visit some day," Kelly invited, smiling at her brother-in-law. "We don't see you often enough."

"I'm not usually in town as much as Pete."

"I don't remember ever seeing Anna Pointer either. Doesn't she ever come to town?"

Joe doubled his hands and slid them into his pockets. "Nope. She has little kids."

"So do I," Kelly said with a laugh.

"I think I hear one now," Joe said, looking up the stairs visible from the kitchen table. In no time, a four-year-old boy came running down the stairs. "Uncle Joe! Uncle Joe, hi! I didn't know you was coming!"

"*Were* coming, son," Kelly said.

Ignoring his mother, the boy continued. "Why are you here? Are you going to give me a ride?"

Joe grinned. Drew was his favorite nephew, mainly because he was the only one old enough to play. He loved it when Joe swung him up on his shoulders and galloped around with him.

Kelly intervened. "No, he's not. But he does have a treat for you," she assured her son.

"What?" Drew asked.

"Uncle Joe is going to drop you off at Granny's house and let you play with a little girl who's coming over. And I want you to be sweet to her."

"A girl? No, Mom, I don't want—"

"Drew?" Pete said quietly.

"Yeah, Dad?"

"Be a gentleman."

"Yes, sir. But girls can't play."

"What do you mean?" Joe asked, curious.

"All Alexandra does is sleep and eat."

Kelly laughed quietly. "That's because she's a baby. She'll do more as she gets older. This little girl is four years old, just like you."

"Okay. Will Granny make cookies?"

Kelly rolled her eyes. "I'm sure she will. She always does."

"Yeah. She's a good granny," Drew said in satisfaction.

"Go put on a clean shirt." He started to protest, but his mother said, "I know you got that shirt out of the dirty clothes. It still has peanut butter on it."

With a disgusted look, he trudged back up the stairs. "I'll be right back, Uncle Joe. Don't leave without me."

"No, I won't."

Kelly sighed. "At least the tornado has passed for a few minutes. He keeps getting more and more energy."

"Yeah. How's Alex doing? Prettier than ever?"

"Of course," Kelly agreed.

"You need kids of your own," Pete said with a frown.

"Don't start, Pete. I'm fine. It gives me time to be a good uncle to Drew."

"I'm not complaining about that, of course, but you're older than me. Don't wait much longer."

Joe shrugged his shoulders and picked up the check and signed lease. "Okay, I'm taking this over to Mrs. Pointer and then driving her into town. I think the payment is due right away."

"And it's okay if I start working the land today?"

"Yep."

"Thanks for lining this up for me, Joe. It will be helpful."

"For me, too. But Anna—that is, Mrs. Pointer, thinks we're giving her charity. I had to talk a little while to convince her I wasn't."

"Good for you," Pete said, watching his brother closely.

"Stop looking at me that way," Joe protested.

"What way?"

"You know what I mean. This is business, that's all."

"Right," Pete said.

"Joe, why don't you bring her by the store and introduce her to us. Lindsay will want to meet her, too."

Joe paused. Then he said, "I might do that. I don't think she has many friends."

"Good. We'll look forward to meeting her."

"Hey, wait a minute. How come you get to meet her and I don't?" Pete demanded of his wife.

She leaned over and kissed him. "Because you have to work today."

Joe laughed at the look on his brother's face. But he wasn't worried. Kelly spoiled Pete, as he spoiled her. They had a good marriage that made Joe envious if he thought about it too long.

His sister, Lindsay, had a good marriage, too. Her husband, Gil Daniels, trained horses and was making quite a name for himself. At least two out of six wasn't bad for his parents. Well, he had to make it three out of six because Logan had married his boss, Abby. A beautiful woman, who talked ranching with the best of them. Logan had learned that the hard way. She was a strong woman who resented being pampered as if she were weak.

But Anna...he thought she might need some pampering. Not that he would be the one to take care of her. He was her temporary protector. Maybe he'd look around for a good man for Anna. He could push her in that direction when he found someone good enough for her. That was a good idea. In town on Saturday, he'd make sure she was introduced around and see who he could find.

In the meantime, he'd think about his friends. Surely he had nice friends who would be interested. Well, not really. Most of his friends were married already. He scratched his head again. There was Dr. Patrick Wilson. He was actually a friend of Pete's. He and Pete had become friends when Kelly took Drew to see him. Joe couldn't hold back a chuckle. They hadn't started out friends. Pete had been too jealous. But he'd delivered Alex and had become a trusted friend. Would Anna—Mrs. Pointer be interested in a doctor? Most women were, he thought with a shrug.

How about Bill Quigley? His wife had died last year. He had a couple of kids too. Anna seemed like a good mom. Maybe that would work out for her. There was Larry Baker. He was a widower, too, but he'd heard some not-so-nice gossip about him.

He wanted to be sure he didn't connect Anna up with someone even worse than Derek. The poor woman had suffered enough. Not that she'd said anything, but her house, while clean, didn't look good. She didn't have any of the frilly stuff like his mom did. And her furnishings looked old. Okay, so he'd make a new list and only include men with a good reputation and good money. It occurred to him that

that list might be pretty short unless he decided to include himself. But, he wasn't looking for marriage. Was he?

When he drove into town early that morning to leave the lease with his lawyer, he actually ran into Patrick Wilson, the man who headed his list for Anna.

"Hey, Pat! What are you doing out this early?"

"Heck, Joe. I'm not out early. I'm just getting back. I had a call about two."

"Everything's okay, I hope," Joe said, a polite hint for more news.

Patrick sighed. "Andy Elkins fell and broke his leg and got a concussion. He'll recover, but it'll take a while."

"Andy? What was he doing up at two in the morning? He's eighty-seven!"

"Making a trip to the bathroom in the dark."

"That's too bad. I guess it's a good thing you don't have a family with the hours you keep," Joe said frowning.

Patrick looked surprised. "I guess you're right. Doctors' marriages aren't too stable from what I've observed. It would take a strong woman to deal with my life."

"Yeah, I guess so," Joe said, thinking he needed to mark Patrick off the list.

Patrick jabbed him with his elbow. "Don't be telling anyone that. You'll ruin my social life."

"I won't," Joe said. He waved goodbye and continued into his lawyer's office. But under his breath he muttered, "I guess we'll see who's next on the list." He had to find a better husband than Patrick. This was going to be hard.

Chapter Three

Julie stayed by the window, anxiously watching for Joe's arrival. Normally, they not only didn't have visitors, but they also didn't go anywhere.

"Mommy! I think he's here. It's a big red truck. Is that what Mr. Crawford drives?"

"I'm not sure. It was dark last night." When she saw Joe get out of the truck, she said, "What a smart little girl you are."

"Can I go out on the porch?"

"Yes, of course, but don't get dirty." Anna went into the baby's room and packed his bag for the day. Lots of diapers and several changes of clothing. "You be good, too, Henry. Okay?" She smiled at the baby and tickled his chin. The little boy cooed and then repeated da-da-da.

"Well, no, not exactly," she whispered as she

picked him up. Great. If Joe Crawford heard Henry's only word, he'd hightail it out of there. She came into the living room just as Julie led Joe inside.

"Mommy, I told Mr. Crawford I liked the cake."

"Good, honey. It was very good, Joe."

"Glad you liked it. Be sure to tell my mom."

"Yes, of course."

"Here's the lease with my and Pete's signatures. Let me hold the baby while you sign it."

"I can put him back in his bed or in the carrier."

"I'll hold him. Julie and I can talk to him, right, Julie?"

"Yes, Mr. Crawford," she agreed, staring at him, as if afraid he might disappear.

He sat down on the couch and whispered something to Julie. She burst into giggles.

"What?" Anna asked, frowning.

"Mommy, he says I can call him Joe!"

"You don't mind?" she asked her guest.

"Nope. I'd prefer it. Where we're going, there are a lot of Mr. Crawfords. We'd get all confused."

Julie gave him a puzzled look. "Why are there lots of Mr. Crawfords?"

"Well, one is my dad. Then I have two more brothers at home and they are Mr. Crawfords, too."

Julie was carefully counting her fingers. "That's four Mr. Crawfords!"

"Wow! I didn't know you were old enough to count. Wait until Drew finds out."

"Who is Drew?" she asked, watching in fascination.

"He's my nephew. He's four, too."

"The same as me!"

"That's right. You're going to play with him today."

Anna had been watching the exchange of words. "Uh, Julie hasn't had anyone to play with. She might not—"

"Don't worry. My mom knows all about breaking up fights. We used to give each other bloody noses all the time." He laughed when Anna stared at him horror-stricken. "Not that Drew and Julie will fight. Don't worry."

Anna was a little apprehensive about Julie spending the afternoon without her supervision. She wasn't used to turning Julie over to someone else. "Of course," she finally said.

Joe actually winked at her. "Stop worrying, Mom. Everything is going to be fine. Oh, by the way, did I mention that my mom makes good cookies?"

"What kind?" Julie asked. "My mom makes good cookies, too."

"Sugar cookies. I think cookie-making's a requirement for all moms. Ready to go?" he asked Anna. Anna knew Joe would never make it in Hollywood as a hero-type, but when he laughed with Julie, he was almost impossible to resist. Foolish thought. He had nothing like that in mind.

"Yes, we're ready. Here's the lease. Give me Henry and I'll put him in his carrier."

"He's a big boy. I'll put him in. He weighs too much for you." He promptly followed his words, as if what he said was true.

"He's not too big for me. I can—"

"Help Julie into the truck. Then you get in and I'll hand you Henry."

Somehow, Anna found herself doing as he ordered. Joe handed in the carrier, grinning at the baby. When Henry broke out into da-da-da, Anna hurriedly said, "That's all he knows how to say."

Joe grinned. "I figured."

Her cheeks flamed.

"Julie, did you bring your storybook? But remember, Mrs. Crawford may not be able to read it to you." She hoped it distracted Joe.

"I bet she will, Julie. That's something my mom likes better than anything. She made sure we all loved to read, too," Joe said.

"Do you have a favorite book?" Julie asked, her eyes wide. "I didn't know Daddies could read."

Joe appeared a bit surprised by Julie's comment. "What?"

"Of course some daddies read, honey. It was just that your daddy was busy."

"What is your favorite storybook?" Julie repeated.

"Peter Pan," Joe said. "I always wanted to fly."

"Me, too!" Julie agreed. "But—but it scared me a little. I didn't want to leave Mommy behind."

"I know what you mean," Joe said, which made Julie happy. It worried Anna. It wouldn't take long for Julie to grow attached to Joe. The poor baby hadn't spent time with her father.

Joe turned off the road to the drive that led to the Crawford homestead. The house was big and well tended.

Before the car stopped, a little boy came out on the front porch.

"Who's that?" Julie asked.

"That's my nephew, Drew. Remember? He's four, too. And he has a little sister about Henry's age."

"A girl baby?"

"Yep. The best kind," Joe assured her.

"Stop trying to charm my little girl," Anna muttered.

Again Joe looked surprised. She said nothing else, unbuckling Henry's carrier.

Mrs. Crawford joined Drew on the porch. Then she stepped down and came toward the truck. "Hello, Anna. Welcome."

"Thank you, Mrs. Crawford. I appreciate your looking after my children this afternoon, but I can take them with me if it will be too much."

"Why no, child. We'll be fine. Drew and Alexandra came over to play with them. We're going to make cookies."

Julie clapped her hands and smiled. "I like cookies."

"I'm glad you do. Come along and I'll introduce you to Drew."

Anna stood there holding her breath, but Julie took Mrs. Crawford's hand and skipped along beside her. The little boy didn't seem nearly as pleased about their plans.

"Don't worry. They'll be fine," Joe whispered in her ear, startling her.

"Come on. I'll carry Henry into the house," he said, grabbing the diaper bag, too.

When they were back in the truck, heading for town, Joe reminded her of her tension. "Why are you so worried about Julie? She's well behaved."

"She's just not used to playing with other children."

"Why not?"

"I don't—I don't have any friends with little kids."

"Your friends don't believe in marriage and children?"

"When I moved here, it was after I married Derek. He didn't run around with married men. So I never met any wives."

"I see."

"I know she'll be fine," she said quietly.

They reached town and Joe took Anna to his lawyer's office. After she signed it, the man said he would copy the agreement and mail her copy. Then, much to her relief, they took the two checks to her bank. She still couldn't believe Joe had made the deposit possible.

"Thank you again, Joe. This is such a relief."

"Good. Oh, my sister and sister-in-law asked us to stop by their store. Do you mind?"

"Of course not." How could she object after all he'd done for her?

When he parked on the main street in front of a big store with the name Oklahoma Chic, she offered to wait in the truck.

"Heck, no. It's you they want to meet, not me. Come on. I won't make you buy anything."

She hoped she could stop herself from shopping. It had been so long since she'd even been in a nice store, much less purchased anything.

When Joe opened the door, cool air conditioning enveloped them. Even though it was only April, Oklahoma warmed up early. There were three ladies in the store, two of them about her age, beautifully dressed, with every hair in place. The other woman was older.

Anna tucked a strand of hair back, hoping she looked even half as nice as those two. She figured they were Joe's sister and sister-in-law.

Joe called to them. "Lindsay, Kelly."

"Joe, you came!" The blond rushed across the store to kiss her brother's cheek, followed by the brunette.

"Lindsay, Kelly, I want you to meet Anna Pointer. She's the one Pete and I are renting land from."

Both ladies smiled, and Kelly offered a hand.

"Come in, Anna. Welcome."

"Thank you," Anna said, feeling awkward. She'd

avoided social situations for so long, she'd almost forgotten how to act. "Your store is lovely."

"Well, it's a lot bigger than when we first started," Kelly said.

"That's because we've added children's clothes," Lindsay said with a chuckle. "That way we can buy our kids' clothes at wholesale."

Anna smiled. "That's a good thing, since they go through them so quickly."

Lindsay nodded and added, "We do consignment here, too. That way you can buy good secondhand clothes at a reduced rate. It saves a lot of money." She led the way to the area where the children's clothes were displayed.

"Some of these clothes come in looking like they've never been worn. I can assure you they're not Drew's," Kelly said with a laugh. "I told him to be a gentleman today."

Anna frowned. "Julie's not used to playing with other children."

Kelly patted her arm. "Don't worry. I talked to Mother Crawford half an hour ago. They're getting along wonderfully well. She's just now putting them down for a nap, so she said don't come back for two hours. We thought maybe you'd join us for lunch."

Anna was startled by Mrs. Crawford's message. "I—I couldn't leave them that long."

Lindsay asked, "Doesn't Julie take a nap every day?"

"Well, yes, of course, but..."

Joe stepped forward. "Anna, if Mom said don't come back for two hours, I'm not brave enough to take you back any sooner. Let's go have lunch."

"We'll just go to the pizza place across the street," Lindsay said.

"But can you leave the store?"

"Oh, we didn't introduce you to Mrs. Carter. She's our manager, and she lives upstairs."

After they performed the introductions, they headed across the street, leaving Mrs. Carter in charge of the store.

Anna couldn't believe what was happening. Her genie had worked another miracle. She hadn't been out to eat with anyone since her marriage. And not anywhere without the kids. One day with Joe, and here she was.

The two women seated themselves together on one side of the table, leaving her to sit with Joe. He even held her chair for her.

"What do you like on your pizza?" he asked.

"Oh, uh, whatever you want."

He gave her a long look, then he said, "Okay, a large pizza with anchovies, and..."

She gasped, but she didn't protest.

Lindsay leaned forward. "Don't worry, Anna, Joe never eats anchovies on his pizza. He's just teasing you."

Joe grinned. "I'm just telling you to make your choices. In our family, you have to stand up for yourself or you'd starve to death."

Anna straightened her spine. "Okay. I like hamburger, Canadian bacon and extra cheese."

"Perfect," Joe said.

The waitress arrived at their table, and he ordered the pizza exactly as Anna had said. Then he ordered a smaller veggie pizza.

Kelly said, "Sometimes we like to eat vegetarian, but today I think I'll have to have meat."

"Not me," Lindsay said. "I'm trying to lose weight after the baby."

"I know what you mean," said Anna. "Henry is nine months old, and I'm still just losing the last of the weight."

Joe leaned back in his chair. He'd filled up on pizza while the ladies talked. He thought Anna was enjoying herself. Somehow, he suspected her late husband had done little to make life easy for her, and she was such a sweetheart.

Yeah, he definitely had to find her a husband, someone who would care for her and her children. Little Julie needed a daddy, and Henry, no, make that Hank, would need one, too. The first thing they had to do was start calling him Hank. He'd be teased to death by the kids if they had to keep calling him Henry.

Women didn't understand these things, but Kelly and Lindsay certainly knew how to put Anna at ease. She hadn't relaxed all day until she met them.

The door to the pizza place opened, and two men

came in. Joe waved them over. Might as well make a start. He stood and extended his hand.

"Hey, Jack, Bob, how are you?"

"Good, Joe. Good to see you," Jack said. "You goofing off today?"

"No, I had to come into town on business. You two know Lindsay and Kelly, don't you?"

The men tipped their hats in their direction.

"Howdy, ladies," Jack said. He considered himself to be a ladies' man.

Bob was a little shy.

"Have you met Anna Pointer?" Joe asked, nodding to Anna.

She smiled at the men. Good start.

"I'm renting some land from Anna. She's a widow, you know." His sister and sister-in-law looked surprised, but he plowed on. "She's got two of the cutest kids you've ever seen, and a hundred and sixty acres that Pete and I are gonna farm."

"Great!" Jack said, looking bewildered.

Joe guessed he was talking too much. Usually he didn't say a lot. He thought about asking them to join them, but he figured the girls were gonna go back to the shop soon, and he wasn't sure Anna would stay there with three men.

"Anna and I are gonna be back in town Saturday to sell produce and things. Stop by and say hello."

Now all three women were staring at him.

Bob said, "At the Farmer's Market?"

"Yeah. Anna's got some things she made besides the fruit and vegetables. She's real handy."

When the two men had walked on, after saying goodbye, Joe sat back down. Anna was still staring at him.

Lindsay said, "You and Anna are going to sell things this weekend?"

"Yeah, she's gonna use Mom's space, and one of us has to be with her."

Lindsay nodded as if she understood perfectly. "Well, maybe we'll drop by, too. We'll be working at the store. Saturday's our busy day, you know."

Soon he and Anna were in the truck on the way back to his mom's place.

"Joe," she said carefully. "You've done so much for me, I—I want you to know I appreciate it. But you don't have to advertise for me."

Joe stared straight ahead. "I want you to get to know people. You live here, you should know everyone."

"That's very nice of you."

"How will you ever meet anyone to marry if you don't get to know everyone?"

Anna stared at him. "What did you say?"

"I said you need to meet people so you can find someone to marry."

Her jaw grew rigid and her eyes flared. "I have no intention of ever marrying again," she explained.

Joe glanced at her, then returned his gaze to the road. "That makes it kinda hard on Julie and Hank."

"What are you talking about? I take good care of my children. And his name is Henry."

"You can't call him Henry, Anna! The other boys will tease him to death."

"There's nothing wrong with the name Henry. It was my father's name!"

"Oh." Joe drove silently. Finally, he said, "Hank's a better name for a boy."

She didn't look at him again. In a hard voice she said, "I appreciate what you've done for me, but that doesn't mean you can take over my life…or my children. If that's what goes along with helping me sell Saturday, forget it."

He waited until he had parked the truck in his mother's front yard. "Anna, you and I both know you need to sell your fruit and vegetables. Saturday you're going whether you like it or not!"

"How dare you!" Anna exclaimed. "And I thought you were so nice!"

"I'm practical," he returned. "No need to cut off your nose to spite your face. Now, go inside and let Mom calm you down." He got out of the truck, slammed the door behind him, and strode toward the barn, hoping his father could do the same for him.

When he entered the barn, he asked his father the question that was uppermost in his mind.

"Dad, why are women so difficult?"

Caleb Crawford looked up from his work mending tack to stare at his son in surprise.

"What are you talking about, Joe?"

"I just explained to this woman that she needed to marry and she got all angry."

"And that surprises you?"

"Yes, it does! It's obvious her children need a father."

"You'd be a good father. Why don't you marry her?" Caleb leaned back on a bale of hay and watched his son's response.

"Damn it, Dad! I told you I wasn't going to marry!"

Caleb burst out laughing.

"What's so funny?" Joe ripped back.

"But I only spoke the truth, son. Why is it making you mad?" Caleb paused then added, "Just like you spoke the truth to Mrs. Pointer."

Joe sighed. His dad was right. Just because it was the truth didn't make it what she wanted. He'd been less than subtle. He was going to have to mend his ways if he was going to convince Anna she should marry.

"You made your point, Dad. I'm right but I can't force my opinion on her."

Caleb started working on the leather again as he asked, "Got any prospects in mind?"

Again, Joe sighed. His father was hitting on every difficulty he'd thought of. "I've been trying to think of someone. First, I thought of Patrick, but he was out all night on a medical call. He wouldn't have much time to spend with her or the kids."

Caleb kept his head down. "No, probably not."

"I ran into a couple of guys in town, but I don't think they'd make good daddies. You know they run around a lot. Kind of like Derek."

"Uh-huh," Caleb nodded.

Irritated, Joe said, "Am I bothering you?"

Caleb looked up, grinning. "Nope, but I don't think this matchmaking stuff ever works out. If it did you would have been married a long time ago."

Joe looked surprised. "Me?"

"Yeah, you," Caleb said. "Your mother thought it would be a good idea. So I'm just warning you. It'll be hard to get her married to someone unless you volunteer."

Joe stood. "Well, I'm not volunteering, but I'm going to find those babies a daddy, and Anna a husband to take care of her, if it's the last thing I do."

Chapter Four

Anna made sure she had everything ready Saturday morning. Joe was right about one thing. She still needed to sell her crop. The fruit and vegetables would rot if she didn't sell them. And the craft items she'd made would bring in good money she could use.

"Mommy, I'm sleepy!" Julie protested, laying her head on the table.

"I know, honey, but you can take a nap later. Mr. Crawford wanted to go early this morning."

"Why do you call him Mr. Crawford? He said they have four Mr. Crawfords."

"Yes, well, there's only one Mr. Crawford who comes here." Thank goodness. The man liked to be in charge!

They both heard the truck. Anna flew to the window. She stared out it, confused when she saw Mrs. Crawford driving Joe's truck.

"Joe's here! Joe's here!" Julie chanted, hopping beside the table.

"No. No, he isn't. His mother is here," Anna said slowly. She went to the front porch, wondering what had happened. "Mrs. Crawford, hello," she called out as the older woman got out of the truck.

"I'm glad you're up. I told Joe it was too early, but he said you'd be ready."

"Yes. Is something wrong with Joe?" Panic was building in Anna's chest, even though she told herself the man meant nothing to her.

"No, of course not. Joe checked his herd this morning before he got ready to leave and he found a cow trying to give birth. He had to stay and pull the calf or possibly lose both the cow and its calf. He called me to take you into town. He'll meet us there as soon as he can."

"Oh, I'm sorry to cause you so much trouble." Anna was embarrassed that this poor woman had to do so much for her.

"Not a problem, child. Come on. Let's get everything loaded in Joe's truck."

After they carried out all the fruit and vegetables, Anna began loading the aprons, quilts, jars of shelled pecans and other oddities she'd thought she could sell.

"Anna, I love these aprons. Where did you get them?" Carol Crawford asked.

"I made them. I thought I'd try to sell the pinafore ones for fifteen dollars. Do you think that's too much?"

"Not at all. I'll gladly pay for one." Carol began

looking at the different styles, some in a solid color and others in nice prints with special trim.

"Mrs. Crawford, I'll gladly give you one for helping me so much."

Carol turned to look at her. "Thank you, Anna. I'll take this one. Now, I want to buy three more. These will make wonderful Christmas presents for my three girls, Abby, Lindsay and Kelly."

"Oh, no, please, take them."

Carol shook her head. "I've accepted your gift, but I will pay for the other three. I have enough cash with me." She opened her purse and took out a fifty-dollar bill. "Here you go. I think the extra five dollars will pay the tax. Now, is Julie ready to go? Drew has been asking to play with her again."

"She enjoyed herself, too," Anna said. She was surprised to have sold three aprons before she even left her driveway. Carol Crawford was a generous woman. Like mother, like son? She thought so.

Once they were all loaded up and in the truck, Carol began the drive to town. "I'm glad Joe is helping you. I warned him that his presence might cause talk, but it didn't seem to bother him."

Anna looked quickly at Carol and then stared out the window. "Especially since he intends to marry me off to some unsuspecting man."

"Ah. I wondered if he'd think of that. He needs to worry about getting married himself. He's not getting any younger."

Anna said nothing.

"You wouldn't want to take him off my hands, would you? He'd make a very good father."

Anna gasped. "Me?"

"Yes, you. I know he's not as handsome as you are pretty, but he's got a good heart." Carol kept her eyes on the road.

I married my handsome husband when I was twenty with stars in my eyes, Anna thought to herself. Now, I'm twenty-six with two children to raise. "Being handsome isn't everything. Mrs. Crawford, Joe is—he's a wonderful man."

"He's a daddy in disguise," Julie added with a big smile.

"What do you mean, Julie?" Carol asked.

"He doesn't look like a daddy, because daddy is big and scary sometimes, but he reads books to me and helps me do things and hugs me, like a real daddy."

"Ah, I see. And he doesn't scare you?"

"Well, he's very big, but that means he can give great piggyback rides."

"Yes, it does. I see you understand him just fine. Perfect!"

"Mrs. Crawford, Joe should find a young lady without a family and make his own. He deserves the best."

"I don't consider a ready-made family to be a detriment, Anna, but the other way would be acceptable, too. If you're not interested in him, maybe you can introduce him to some other ladies while you're selling everything. He's sure he's too ugly to attract a woman."

Anna said nothing and Carol turned to look at her. Anna quickly wiped away her slack-jawed look. Not sure she heard correctly, she said, "Joe thinks he's too ugly?"

"That's what he said. High school was hard for him. He doesn't realize how much he's changed since then, and nothing we say can convince him."

"How ridiculous! He's—he's wonderful when he smiles. And such a gentleman." She thought about his behavior on Thursday, but he really was a gentleman in spite of losing his temper.

"See what you can do to convince him of that," Carol suggested with a warm chuckle.

Anna almost agreed, but then she realized the problem. She couldn't convince Joe that he was attractive to *her,* or he'd think she wanted him. That would be the wrong message, she told herself firmly.

"I'll introduce him to any ladies I know," she agreed, staring straight ahead, not noticing Carol's delighted smile.

Joe arrived at the Farmer's Market about eight-thirty, after delivering a new calf and putting the mother and baby in the barn. Then he'd had a quick shower and redressed. He couldn't turn up all dirty. He found his mother and Anna in the correct space, enjoying themselves. It was Julie who spotted him first. She jumped to her feet and screamed "Joe!" running to him.

He swooped her up into his arms and she screamed again with delight.

"I think my son must've arrived," Carol said with a chuckle.

"Yes, I believe he has," Anna agreed, her gaze pinned on the tall man.

"Hi, Mom, Anna. Sorry I'm late," Joe said.

Anna dismissed his apology and his mother said she was having fun. Julie, back on the ground, tugged on his shirt. "Do you have a baby calf?"

"I do, sweetheart. He's about the same size as you."

"Can I see him?"

"Sure. On the way home today, we'll go by my place and you can pet him. Okay?"

"Yes!" Julie said, dancing around in excitement. "Mommy. Joe's going to let me pet his calf."

"How nice of Joe. But he might be too tired today. We'll see."

Joe winked at Julie. "Moms worry too much. I won't be too tired."

Julie beamed at him, while Anna wanted to curse a blue streak. Which she never did. But her husband had taught her a few words before his death. Instead, she sighed.

"How are sales going?" he asked the two ladies.

"Very well," Carol said. "She's already sold three of the quilts she's brought."

"Yes, but I sold them to you!" Anna pointed out. "And three aprons, too."

"Yes, but you sold all the other aprons, too. I'm glad I made my choices first," Carol added, smiling.

"You didn't buy me an apron, did you Mom?" Joe asked, a grin on his face.

"No, I didn't, though it would've been a good idea. You could start a hope chest for a future bride."

He turned beet-red. "Mom!" he warned in a stern voice.

"It's time I leave you two to sell the rest of this stuff and go fix lunch for the children."

Anna wanted to plead for her to stay a little longer, but she'd already imposed on Joe's mother more than she'd intended. She hugged Julie goodbye and made sure Henry's diaper was dry. Then she watched as Carol and the two children got in her car and headed for home.

"Don't look so forlorn," Joe whispered in her ear. "They'll be fine."

Anna turned around and settled in the garden chair she'd brought to sit on. "I know they will be," she answered sturdily and whisked away the lone tear that had escaped.

She prayed for a lot of customers, not for the sales but to keep her and Joe busy. She didn't want any heart-to-hearts with him.

Then, a lady she knew walked by and stopped suddenly to stare at her. Anna had met her a long time ago when she'd first married.

"Anna? Anna Pointer? Is that you? I wasn't even sure you still lived here. How are you doing?"

Since the woman's gaze was focused on Joe, Anna knew it wasn't herself who inspired the enthusiasm.

But she'd promised to introduce Joe to any women she knew.

"I'm fine, Louise. Have you met Joe Crawford?"

"Of the famous Crawfords?" Louise gushed, blinking her lashes at Joe. "I'm delighted to meet you Joe." She introduced her friends to him, also, ignoring Anna.

As Joe greeted each of the other ladies, Louise leaned closer to Anna. "You're certainly doing well for yourself, snagging a Crawford!"

Anna started to protest, but she was afraid Joe would overhear. "Joe's helping me sell my fruits and vegetables." She moved to wait on an older lady who was looking at her tomatoes. "May I help you, ma'am?"

"Are these organically grown?"

"I didn't use any fertilizer on them, if that's what you mean."

"Well, they're just wonderful. How much for this little basket?"

Anna told her and then took the money the lady offered. She put the tomatoes in a sack. Her tomatoes were doing well. She moved back to her chair only to find Louise sitting there, flirting with Joe.

"Here, Anna, take my chair. I'll sit on the end of the truck," Joe said, jumping up at once. Since the tailgate had been let down, there was plenty of room for Joe, but it put him farther away from Louise.

"I don't want to interrupt your conversation. I'll sit on the end of the truck."

He refused again, but she stubbornly went to the

back of the truck. Before she could sit down, however, he spanned her waist with his hands and lifted her into place. Surprised, she blushed bright red. "Th-Thank you."

"Anna, did you slave away on a quilt to sell?" Louise interrupted. "I've heard they're frightfully expensive. Of course, I don't suppose you have much social life with two kids, so you'd have plenty of time."

"Yes."

"What size is it?"

"King-size," she said, hoping it wasn't a size Louise wanted. She'd hate to sell to her, but she couldn't afford to turn it down.

"Oh, too bad. I have a queen-size bed. Don't you have any others?"

"I did, but I've already sold them."

After a brief silence, Louise whispered something to Joe and then stood. "I guess I'd better go catch up with my friends." She reached up and patted Joe's cheek. "I'll see you later, Mister."

Anna thought if she hadn't been there, Louise might even have kissed him. And he thought he was unattractive to women? How ridiculous could he be?

Without a word, Joe lifted Anna from the truck and put her in her chair, as if she were two years old.

"Joe! I can move on my own!"

"I guess you can. But I wasn't sure you would."

She pressed her lips tightly together. He changed the subject and caught her by surprise.

"How much is that king-size quilt?"

"Five hundred dollars. I don't really expect to sell it, but king-size are hard to find so—"

"Sold!"

Anna stared at him, her eyes wide with shock. "What?"

"You just sold it. Pete bought one for Kelly at the fair a couple of years ago and I've been wanting one ever since, but I have a king-size bed. I did find one that size but it was pink and yellow. Not exactly a guy's colors."

Anna had chosen navy, yellow and white because she figured the colors had to be right for a man. Most women alone wouldn't have a king-size bed. "But Joe, your mother bought the other quilts and I—"

"That has nothing to do with me. Do you want a check or shall I go to the bank and get cash?"

"Of course I can take your check, Joe! What a ridiculous question!"

He grinned as he wrote out a check. "I'm excited to find this quilt." After he handed her the check, he rubbed the quilt and opened it up a fold or two to see the pattern. "What's the pattern called?"

"You're going to want your money back when I tell you," she mumbled.

"Why?"

"Because it's called the wedding ring quilt."

"Oh. Well, there's no law against a bachelor using that pattern, is there?"

"Of course not. And anyone seeing you with Louise would figure it would be completely appropriate in three months...or maybe sooner."

"You jealous because the woman flirted with me?"

"No, but your mother said—" She suddenly closed her mouth, not sure she should reveal Carol's conversation.

"Don't pay any attention to my mother. She believes all her little chicks are perfect."

"I don't see how she can use the word little for any of you but Lindsay, and she's tall."

"Good point."

They had a steady stream of customers for the next hour or two. Anna was making a lot of money. Again Joe had brought her good luck. Most of the men stopped to talk to Joe, and their wives looked at her goods to pass the time. She wouldn't have sold nearly as much without Joe there. She couldn't have even used the spot without Joe. Julie thought he was a daddy in disguise, but she thought he was her lucky charm.

Joe was glad Anna was raking in the bucks. All of the things she'd made had sold out early. It was almost one o'clock and his stomach was rumbling. "I'm going to get us some lunch. Barbecue sandwiches okay with you?"

She nodded to him and continued with her sales. Joe slipped away, a smile on his face. She was a hard worker. And she never let down her guard. Everyone else was beginning to see them as a couple, Joe had been fending off the teasing all morning, but Anna didn't seem to notice.

He got the sandwiches and a couple of colas and

headed back. Too bad they couldn't close some door and enjoy lunch together. Anna would insist on—he came to an abrupt halt. Then he jogged down the row of sellers. Anna was trying to pull her arm away from a man standing way too close to her.

Joe set the food on the back of the truck and put an iron grip on the man's arm. The other man jerked around, a look of surprise on his face, and Joe saw it was one of her husband's old buddies. "Getting a little too friendly, Bud. Seems to me the lady was protesting."

"Hey, Joe, I wasn't hurting anyone."

"I think you were."

"Well, who asked you? Anna and I are old friends."

"Really? Anna, did you want Bud to get so friendly?"

"No, I didn't. I want him to go away." She said those words quietly, but firmly.

"You heard the lady," Joe said.

"I should've known. You'd win every time, Joe. Since you got the Crawford millions behind you." With that ugly remark, Bud wrenched his arm from Joe's hold and strode down the aisle.

Anna had turned her back to Joe, he suspected to hide her tears, and he turned her around by gently touching her shoulders. "Are you all right?" he asked.

"Yes! Yes, I'm fine," she assured him but he noticed she didn't look at him. He wrapped his arms around her and held her close. "It's all right honey. I won't let anyone hurt you."

She didn't pull away immediately, and he relished their closeness. She smelled of sweet flowers and felt like soft silk. He didn't ever want to let go.

She finally pulled away. "I'm sorry. I—I panicked. He tried to get fresh when my husband was alive. I was afraid nothing would stop him now."

"I'll make sure he doesn't touch you again."

"That's not necessary, Joe. Besides, it would make people think—I mean, it would look like—you can't do that, Joe."

"Ah-uh," he said stubbornly. Then he turned around and got their lunch, handing her a sandwich and cola.

"This tastes good, Joe. I didn't realize how hungry I was. Otherwise I wouldn't have panicked," she told him several minutes later.

He grinned. She was trying to disguise her fright. She was some little lady!

"Of course not. You know, another hour and I think you will have sold everything."

"Yes, isn't it wonderful? I never dreamed I'd do so well. And I owe it all to you."

"Nonsense! You just needed to have an opportunity to sell it. I think you could sell some of these men a snowman in hell, if their wives weren't with them."

"Joe! That's not true and don't ever say that in front of Julie!"

"Of course not. She's the sweetest thing! Of course, Hank will be a lot of fun when he gets a little older. Pete plays ball with Drew. He wants him to go to Oklahoma State on a football scholarship if he can."

"Football? Henry will never play such a dangerous sport. He might get hurt."

"You're right, Henry won't. But Hank might," Joe said with a big grin.

"Joe Crawford, I told you we weren't going to call him Hank."

"Aw, Anna, you're going to ruin the boy's life!"

"I most certainly will not!"

Another customer came by and Joe sat back and finished his sandwich while Anna sold the last of her produce.

"I guess we can go as soon as you finish your lunch," he said. "That will give us plenty of time to go by my place and see the calf. You can help me put the quilt in place, too. I can't wait to put it on my bed."

She agreed with reluctance, but he wasn't going to disappoint Julie just because her mother was reluctant to spend time with him. He'd promised.

The children were still napping when they reached the Crawford homestead. Joe sprawled at his mother's table, eating chocolate cake, while Anna and his mother discussed other things Anna could make to sell the next time she went to the market.

"I'd like to go again next week, and this time I can pay the fee, thanks to you and Joe, so I won't have to bother you."

"You'll do no such thing," Joe muttered, not looking up.

"Why not?" Anna challenged him.

Joe only spoke one word. He knew it wasn't fair, but it was the truth. "Bud."

Anna said nothing, keeping her gaze fixed on the table.

"Bud who?" Carol asked, her gaze flying between the two of them.

Joe looked up. "I think his last name is Daugherty. He's an old friend of her husband's."

"What did he do?"

"He grabbed her in spite of her protests. I don't know what else he would've done because I got back with our lunches."

"My goodness, child. Joe's right."

"No, really, I'll be all right."

"Of course you will," Joe said amiably, "because I'll be right beside you, like it or not."

Chapter Five

They argued all the way to Joe's house. However, Anna realized her arguing was upsetting her little girl. "We have to stop this," she muttered under her breath to Joe, nodding in Julie's direction.

"Good. Because no matter how many fees you pay, I'll still be there, taking care of you. I feel responsible for you."

Anna sighed. "Don't you realize how many people thought we were…together?"

"Don't worry. I'll get the word out. Now, Julie, are you ready to go see the calf?"

"I can still see it?" Julie asked tentatively.

Joe seemed surprised. "Of course, you can. I promised."

"But I thought you were mad at Mommy."

"Your mother is stubborn, that's all. I need to keep her safe. But that has nothing to do with what I promised you. Come on, I'll give you a piggyback ride to the barn.''

Julie's worried look disappeared and she leaped from the truck into Joe's arms. Anna knew she should be frustrated with Joe, but anyone who could put that look of delight on Julie's face couldn't be all bad. Besides, if Bud came back around and she was alone, she'd have to cause a scene to get him to leave her alone. And she would, though but she'd rather avoid one.

She picked up Hank—she meant Henry—and followed the other two. He seemed to be in a good mood, babbling and smiling. ''Did he charm you too, Henry? For a man who thinks he doesn't attract women, he's mighty smooth.''

''You talking to me?'' Joe called back, still a few steps ahead of her and her baby.

''No, I was talking to the baby.'' She avoided using his name because she certainly wasn't going to accidentally slip and call him Hank in front of Joe.

In the barn, Joe put Julie on the rails of the gate leading into one of the stalls, warning her to hold on as he opened the gate.

The cow moved, exposing her baby to their eyes.

''Don't let her step on you!'' Julie screamed.

''I'm safe, Julie, but you must be quiet so we don't upset the new mama. This is her first baby.'' He patted the cow on her neck, speaking quietly to her. Then he bent over and scooped the wobbly calf into his arms and carried it to the gate where Julie waited.

"What do you think?" he asked Julie as she reached out to touch the baby animal.

"She's so cute! Mommy, can I have one?" Julie pleaded as she stroked the red-brown coat of the calf.

"No, sweetie, you can't. We don't know how to take care of cows."

"Don't you even have a milk cow?" Joe asked, surprised.

"No. Derek wasn't interested in taking care of any animals. And he didn't drink milk."

"I think Dad's got too many milk cows. I'll see what he wants for one of them."

His casual take-charge attitude irritated her. "Don't do that on my account, because I won't be buying a milk cow."

"But you buy milk, don't you? It will make life easier for you to go to the barn and get your milk than to drive into town."

"Joe, I don't know how to milk a cow, or take care of it, or what to do with the milk once I've gotten it."

"Heck, I can teach you all that." He set the calf down and opened the gate. "Come on, Julie, we're going to teach your mommy all about cows."

Anna stood there in shock as Joe and her daughter left the barn the way they'd come in.

"Wait! I'm not buying a milk cow." Her protest didn't affect Joe's plans. In only a few minutes, she found herself in another stall with a calm cow and Joe. He'd put Henry back in his carrier and set him on a bale of hay. Then he'd ordered Julie to keep an eye on him. Next, he took Anna's hand and pulled her into the stall after him.

"Joe, have you listened to me at all? I don't want to milk a cow. It—it looks disgusting. And I wouldn't know what to do with the milk after I got it."

"I'll show you," he said, as if that settled everything.

He plopped a stool down beside the cow and placed an aluminum can under her udder. "It's real simple, Anna. You take one of her teats between your thumb and your forefinger, and you gently squeeze it." A stream of milk hit the can, making a startling noise. "After you get good, you can do two at a time. That way it doesn't take as long."

"I like buying my milk from the store."

He ignored her and stood. "Now sit down. I'm going to stay right here beside you. So don't worry."

He put his hand on her shoulder and she sat, since she didn't have a choice.

"Now, take a teat and squeeze down it. Gently. Old Bessie is well-trained."

Anna couldn't believe she was milking a cow, but a sense of pride filled her as she heard the milk hitting the can.

"Hey! You're a natural!" Joe exclaimed. He opened the gate and allowed Julie to come in for a minute to see her mother milk.

"Okay, I can do it, but I really don't want a milk cow, Joe. Truly."

"Hmmm, we'll give you some time to get used to

the idea. Finish milking Bessie. She'll be upset if she doesn't get rid of all that milk tonight.''

To Anna's amazement, she actually got good enough to milk two teats at once and soon had the bucket about two-thirds full.

''That will do it, Anna. That's about what she gives twice a day. Now, let's take it in the house and I'll complete your education.''

He took the bucket from her, hung up the stool, and then picked up Henry's carrier with his free hand. ''Come along, ladies. We're heading for the kitchen.''

Anna loved his house. It had been recently built and the kitchen had all the latest appliances. She got distracted just wishing she had half the room and all the equipment he had. ''Your kitchen is lovely.''

''Thanks. Mom helped me figure out what I'd need. And Lindsay and Kelly advised me on how to decorate.''

All through the lessons on what to do with the fresh milk, she kept studying the kitchen.

''Are you listening to me?''

Anna jumped and then looked sheepishly up at him. ''Not really. I'm admiring your kitchen. Or maybe I should say turning green with jealousy.''

''Want to help me cook dinner?''

She blinked several times. ''What did you say?''

''I'm thinking someone might fall asleep without her supper if I take you home now. I guess I got carried away about the milking. You must be tired, too. So we can cook dinner here and feed Julie and maybe even Hank, and then take them home.''

"Oh, no, that's too generous of you, Joe," she protested.

"Nope. You put up with my bossiness act and I know I was wrong. Let me make it up to you by fixing dinner." He grinned, and Anna couldn't have refused him anything. Besides, she always admired anyone who could admit when he was wrong.

Joe took Julie into the den and turned on the television. He put Hank down beside her and told her to call if the baby got unhappy. Then he came back in and pulled some dishes out of the refrigerator.

"Mom made this meat loaf for me. We can heat it up, make some mashed potatoes and I'll open a can of green beans. I think I have a package of rolls in here we can bake, and that will make a good dinner. Can Hank eat mashed potatoes?"

"Yes, and I have some baby food in his bag. I put it in for lunch and I doubt that he ate it all."

"Great."

They worked well together, and dinner was on the table in about twenty minutes. Joe brought the children in. Julie looked like she might've gone to sleep, but Anna didn't ask. She held Henry in her lap, since there was no high chair, and fed him, while Joe fixed Julie's plate. It was so unusual for Anna to have help with the children. She could tell Julie liked it, too.

"Joe, I can't thank you enough," she said after putting Henry in his carrier and filling her own plate.

"Aw, come on, Anna. You know you were ready to beat me to a pulp when I insisted you milk the cow." He gave her a sheepish look.

"Well, you are rather dictatorial," she admitted, grinning.

"I'm the oldest, you know. I always feel I have to help people and—I worry about what you'll do if I'm not there to help you."

She actually sniffed. "I'll manage, Joe. I've taken care of my children so far. I'll admit you've been there for me in the last few days and I appreciate it, but I can't get used to having help all the time."

"Don't worry. I'm thinking about who will make a good husband for you and a daddy to Julie and Hank."

Anna rolled her eyes. "Your mom said you should worry about a bride for yourself. I'm supposed to introduce you to every woman I know. But I don't know too many."

"Good. No one's going to want to marry me, except people like Louise, who thinks she'll have all the money she wants if she marries me."

"But Joe—" she began to protest, though she knew that was on Louise's mind. "Well, maybe you're right about Louise, but you have a lot to offer a woman."

Joe laughed. "You spent too much time with Mom this morning."

She protested, but he ignored whatever she said. Instead, he turned his attention to Julie. "Are you exhausted, sweetheart?"

She nodded. "But I had fun. What are you going to name the baby cow?"

"Well, I haven't decided. Would you like to name her? She's a girl, you know."

"How do you know?" Julie asked.

For the first time that day, Joe was at a loss for words. He gave Anna a panicky look.

In response to his silent plea, Anna said, "Joe knows how to tell which is which. When you're older he can show you, but you're too young now. Just take his word for it."

Julie nodded and looked at Joe with new respect. "Okay. Can we name her Rosy?"

"Rosy? I think that's a great name. Rosy she is!"

Julie clapped her hands. "Thank you, Joe."

"You have great manners, Julie. You're welcome. Now, let's get you home so you can be tucked into bed."

"We have to do the dishes first, Joe," Anna said, appalled that he would walk off and leave the dishes on the table.

"Nah. I'll put the leftover food away and we can stack the dishes in the sink. My cleaning lady comes in the morning."

"You have a cleaning lady?" Anna couldn't help thinking about what a change that would make in her life.

"Yeah. I'm too busy with the cows and all. Julie, will you bring me the butter?" he asked as he stood. In no time, everything was put away and the dishes stacked in the sink. "Nice job, Julie, and Mommy, too. Even Hank was good, drifting off to sleep without complaining."

"That's because he filled up on your mashed potatoes," Anna told him. "I think he may sleep all night tonight."

"Good, 'cause you're looking a little tired, too. Maybe you'll get to sleep late."

He swung Julie up on one hip and picked up the carrier with his free hand and led the way to his truck. Anna felt strange only carrying the diaper bag. Usually she juggled several things, along with the baby and making sure Julie followed.

He drove them home as the moon rose and Anna felt a satisfaction she hadn't felt in a long time. "Thank you, Joe, for all you've done for us. There's no way I can repay you." Then she remembered. "Oh, Joe, we didn't put your quilt on your bed! I'm so sorry. I forgot!"

"It's all right, Anna. I can do that when I get home. And maybe tomorrow you can come see how it looks."

"Not tomorrow. That would be too much trouble, but in a few days, when you won't be so tired of us, we'll come see it."

"Okay, whenever you're ready."

Anna didn't speak again. She was afraid she'd beg him to insist on tomorrow. But at least she'd know he had something she'd made to sleep with. Somehow that made her feel better.

The next morning, Julie's first question of the day was about Joe.

"When is Joe coming?"

Anna, ready to dish up the oatmeal, almost dropped the pan. "What are you talking about, Julie? Joe's not coming to see us today."

"We didn't get to see our quilt on his bed. He said we could see it today."

"I know, sweetie, but I told him we wouldn't come over today. He's had to spend too much time with us the last few days."

"But he likes for us to spend time with him."

"He's not coming over today. Do you want raisins in your oatmeal?"

Julie sank back in her chair and crossed her small arms over her chest. "I want to see Joe."

Anna had known Julie liked Joe. It was hard not to like him with his big grin and his gentle warmth with the children. "Julie, Joe isn't kin to us. He just helped out a few times. He has his own life."

Julie glowered at her. "Don't you like Joe?"

"Of course I do. And that's why we can't hang on to him. Because we like him, we have to find him a lady to marry so he can have his own children."

"But I want to be Joe's children."

Anna turned her back on her stubborn daughter. "No, Julie. That's not going to happen. Let's go to church this morning. You would be in a Sunday School class with lots of children your age. Drew might even be there."

Anna was pleased when her distraction worked. She'd been thinking about going back to church. Derek had refused to attend church when they'd married. She'd attended a few times, but it was awkward to go without her husband.

For Julie's sake, she'd try again.

She dressed Julie in her best dress and put her hair

in a ponytail. Then she did the best she could with Henry. For herself, she picked out an old dress that still looked good. Then she loaded the children in her ramshackle truck and, after a minute or two, got it started.

Halfway there, the truck engine abruptly shut down. She coasted to the side of the road so she wouldn't block other cars.

"Why are we stopping, Mommy?" Julie asked.

"The car stopped, sweetie. And I don't know how to fix it."

"We should call Joe. He'll come rescue us."

"We don't have a phone." Anna tried to start the truck, but nothing happened. A car pulled up beside them. "Need some help?" the woman asked.

"Are you going into town?" Anna questioned. "If so, could you ask the garage to send someone out?"

"Are they open on Sunday?"

Anna didn't know. But at least she knew she could pay for the help, thanks to Joe.

"Oh. Probably not. Well, thanks anyway."

The woman drove off.

Anna sat there for a few minutes, until Julie got tired of waiting and began to fidget. That stirred Anna to action.

"Well, Julie my girl, I guess we'd better start walking home." Fortunately they'd only come a mile or two.

"We're going to walk home? But I want to go to Sunday School."

"I'm sorry, baby. We can't today. Maybe next Sunday, after I get the truck fixed."

She wished she hadn't given in to her ego and worn high heels. It was going to make the trek back home more difficult. She got out and came around to Julie's side and opened the door. "Hop out, Julie. I'll carry Henry. Can you carry the diaper bag?"

Julie nodded, but she added, "I wish Joe was here. He could carry me and the bag."

"We're strong, baby. We can take care of ourselves. Oh, look. There's a butterfly. Let's count all the butterflies we see on the way home. Whoever gets the most will win."

"What will I win, Mommy?"

"How about the last piece of the cake Mrs. Crawford sent us?"

"Okay," Julie said cheerfully, easily distracted.

Fifteen minutes later, Julie wasn't looking for butterflies. She was complaining that her feet hurt. She wanted her mother to carry her, too. Anna knew she couldn't carry Julie. Her arms ached from carrying Henry, and they weren't even halfway home. They heard another vehicle and scooted to the side of the road. She kept Julie moving, hoping they could cover more land while she was watching the truck.

"It's a red truck, Mommy. Maybe it's Joe!"

"No, sweetie. It's probably not. Now come along."

When the truck came to a halt beside them and a familiar voice greeted them, even Anna was thrilled to greet Joe Crawford. "Hello, Joe."

"Don't you know walking on the road is dangerous? I saw your truck back there. What happened?"

"It stopped."

He leaned across the front seat and opened his passenger door. "Come on, get in."

In spite of her exhaustion, she refused. "We don't want to take you out of your way, Joe. We'll be okay."

Julie, however, was already scrambling into the front seat.

"Julie! Get down. We're not going with Joe."

Joe was smiling. "Don't be so hardheaded, Anna. Come on."

She hesitated and finally said, "All right, but you can just run us back to our house."

"Nope. You're all dressed up for church. We can make it back in time for the sermon after we put the kids in the nursery so they can have a good time."

"Joe, we can't go to church together. People will think—"

"We'll tell them different." He held out a hand to help her and she gave in. He took Henry in his big arms and she climbed up to set beside Julie.

"Fasten your seat belt, Mommy."

"Yeah, Mommy. Fasten your seat belt," Joe said with a grin.

Anna did so and sat silently while Joe drove them back to the church. She didn't have a way home after church, either. And she didn't want to be seen leaving the church with him. That was sure to cause talk.

"Is the garage open today?"

"Don't think so. I'll get someone out to look at it tomorrow."

"I'll take care of it, thank you."

He gave her a funny look and turned his attention to Julie, ignoring Anna the rest of the way into town.

Chapter Six

Anna knew she'd been right when all the heads turned as Joe guided them into church. There was a lot of whispering. She leaned toward him. "Joe, everyone's whispering."

"I told you I'd take care of it. After the sermon I'll introduce you to some nice guys."

Anna rolled her eyes. Great, everyone would think she'd come to church to find a man. "Joe, I don't want a husband."

"Anna, you have to think of Julie and Hank. They need a daddy."

Thank goodness Julie was in the Sunday School and hadn't heard that. Joe ushered her into a row filled with Crawfords, as if she were part of the family. That wasn't going to make people think she was just a friend. When the service ended, Anna thought maybe she could get a ride from Pete and Kelly, but Joe took her elbow, guiding her towards the nursery.

"Joe," she whispered. "Maybe Pete and Kelly will give me a ride so you won't have to bother."

He dropped her arm and stepped away. He frowned at her. "You hate being seen with me that much?"

The bitterness in his voice made her believe what his mother had said about him for the first time. "I'm trying to protect you, Joe."

He stared at her. "What are you talking about?"

"You aren't going to find someone to marry if you're always helping me."

"You're crazy," Joe said.

"I am not. Your mother said I should introduce you to other women."

Joe shook his head. "Okay, my mother's the crazy one. Let's go get the kids."

Anna gave up. She was afraid if she didn't go get the kids they would get upset. She needn't have worried; Julie was happy because Drew was there and Joe would be there to get her. Then they went to the nursery to get Henry. Joe greeted the lady working there.

"Hey Sally, we're here to get Hank."

She gave him a confused look.

"His name is Henry," Anna said.

"Yeah, but we're calling him Hank."

Anna wanted to protest again, but Sally had already headed for the bed where Henry was sleeping. She carried him over to them and added, "Hank was a very good boy."

Joe laughed. "Of course he was."

"Well, he certainly doesn't take after you, Joe," Sally teased.

Anna kept quiet. She figured to comment would only call attention to her being with Joe. When they turned around, she almost ran into Kelly. "Kelly, can you give me and my kids a ride home? My truck broke down."

"Well, sure, but Mother Crawford said you were coming to lunch."

"Oh, no. We can't do that," Anna said.

"But Sunday lunch is tradition," Kelly said.

"It's family tradition, but we're not family."

Julie looked up. "You mean I can play with Drew some more?"

Joe scooped Julie up into his arms. "Of course you can."

"Joe," Anna protested.

"Come on, Anna. It'll be a treat for Julie." Anna knew she had lost control.

With a sigh, Anna asked one last time, "Are you sure your mother won't mind?"

"She'll be delighted."

And of course, Anna ended up in his truck on the way to his parents' house.

Since everyone there would be family, she assumed they'd understand there was nothing romantic about lunch. Until Julie started talking.

"Joe," Julie began. "Mommy says you want to have children."

"Julie, don't," Anna said with a gasp. She knew what was coming next.

"Why not?" Joe asked.

"It's too personal," Anna said.

"If you know, why can't Julie know?"

Anna closed her eyes. Julie, as she'd expected, replied, "I'd like to be your little girl."

"I'd like that, too, sweetheart. But I don't know if Hank would like it."

"Yes, he would," Julie insisted.

"Julie," Anna said sternly. "You can't ask to be Joe's daughter."

"Why not?"

"You just can't. And don't say another word about it."

Julie glared at her mother, but Anna didn't smile at her child. She'd embarrassed her.

After lunch had ended, Anna joined the other women in the kitchen and immediately apologized to Joe's mother.

"Never you mind, Anna. It didn't upset me. In fact, I think that's a wonderful idea."

"Mrs. Crawford!" Anna protested, scandalized. "But I promised I would help Joe find a wife."

"Yes, I know dear. But I think I should have enlisted Julie. She's had the best idea yet."

Anna blushed a bright red. "I—I thought I'd ask Kelly and Lindsay to help me. I don't know too many women."

"You think it's because Joe doesn't know anyone?" His mother asked. "Heck, he knows everyone in the county, but you're the only one he's taken any interest in.''

''He's…just helping me.''

''But Anna,'' Lindsay said. ''Don't you see? I've never seen Joe so happy. It's as if he really is Julie's daddy.''

Anna gave up. She industriously dried the dishes as Mrs. Crawford washed them. When Lindsay and Kelly began talking about their store, she relaxed. When the dishes were done, Anna thanked Mrs. Crawford for having her children to lunch. Then she hurried out before Joe's mother could explain why it was good. She didn't need his mother matchmaking.

''Joe, we finished the dishes. Could you take me home now?''

Joe didn't seem in any hurry. He was holding Hank, she meant Henry, playing with him. She didn't see her daughter. ''Where's Julie?'' she asked before Joe answered.

''She went to show Drew the calf. Rosy.''

''By themselves?''

Pete laughed. ''Anna, honey, you worry about them going to the barn by themselves when they're fifteen, not now.''

The men all laughed except for Mr. Crawford. ''Don't mind their teasing, Anna.''

Anna smiled at him, grateful for his comment. Then she said she was going to get Julie because they were going to go home if Joe didn't mind taking them.

Joe stood. ''I'll go with you, Anna.''

''Thank you,'' she said softly. She was glad he was

going with her until he slung his arm around her shoulders.

"Joe!" She whispered. "What are you doing?"

He put on the innocent look she'd seen before.

"I'm just walking you to the barn, Anna."

"With your arm around me!" she exclaimed.

"Are you afraid I'll drop Hank?"

"No, but—oh, never mind."

Joe pulled her closer. "I've got an idea that may fix everything. We'll talk later."

Anna couldn't imagine what he meant....

Joe drove Anna and her children home a couple of hours later. Mrs. Crawford had several things to keep them longer, but Anna finally insisted. As soon as they reached the house, she sent Julie up for a nap and put Henry down for his, which would clear the way for some private talking.

As soon as she came back into the other room she asked, "What did you think of that will make everything okay? What?"

"Let me ask you a question first," Joe said.

"Ask me a question?"

"Yeah. Were you in love with Derek?"

That was the last thing Anna had thought he would ask. And difficult to answer... "Why do you want to know?" she challenged.

"Because I get the idea you don't intend to remarry."

"Of course I don't intend to remarry. Why would I?"

"And that's why I asked that question. Why did you marry him if you didn't love him?"

She turned her back to him, hoping to avoid him seeing her tears. "I thought he loved me and I was alone. My parents had just died and I wanted someone to love me. It was wrong, but I paid for it and I won't do it again."

"You know, your children need a father," he said.

"Quit saying that! They're doing just fine, no thanks to Derek."

"I agree, except that Julie wants to be my little girl."

"Tomorrow she'll probably want you to be Santa Claus. Little girls change." She couldn't believe he looked hurt. But he did and she felt badly.

"Joe, I didn't mean to hurt your feelings. You would be a wonderful father. But you don't have to marry a widow who already has children."

A thought suddenly occurred to her. Oh no! What if Joe couldn't have children? She hadn't thought of that before.

"What?" Joe asked staring at her.

"Can—can you have children?"

The worried look on Joe's face disappeared, replaced by sexy chuckles that sent shivers down her back. He suddenly pulled her against him, waggled his eyebrows and asked, "I've never tried. Should we give it a go now?"

"Joe Crawford! I can't believe you would say such a thing." She pushed away from him, afraid he would notice how much she enjoyed his touch.

"So, now you know my idea," Joe said with a teasing grin.

"But I said I didn't want to marry."

"But you're going to have to. Your children need a father. And you need a husband."

"Now wait just a minute, Joe. I can take care of my children and myself."

"You're doing okay, but this is a tough world. And just every once in a while wouldn't you like to put your head on my shoulder and let me do the hard stuff?"

She couldn't admit how appealing that picture was. "No."

He sighed. "Lady, you are so stubborn. Let me say it in black and white. I haven't married because most women only want to marry me for my money. They think I'm ugly."

"Joe, that's ridiculous!"

"No, it's not. But you don't seem to mind my looks. And Julie's not afraid of me and Hank, well, he just plain doesn't know any better."

"Of course he doesn't, because you're not ugly. You're a warm, kind man."

"Yeah, just go ahead and say I have a great personality. I know what that means."

Anna was so frustrated she doubled up her fist and slugged him in the shoulder.

Joe responded, too. He pulled her against his chest and kissed her.

Anna didn't sleep well that evening. She couldn't get her mind off Joe's suggestion. How absurd! Yet tempting, to let Joe help her solve her problems for the rest of her life. Except she'd be doing what he'd accused other women of doing, marrying for money. Joe didn't deserve that.

Marrying Joe for what he could provide wouldn't even be the worst thing about his idea. She had never enjoyed sex with Derek. He had made no effort to please her, or even to teach her how to please him. Derek had taken what he wanted and abandoned her. That was what she had come to expect from men. Joe, with one kiss, however, had taught her differently. The kiss had been tender, loving, patient. And made her want to kiss him again. She was shocked by that reaction.

And she wondered how he had reacted. He probably slept like a baby. Maybe he'd give up the idea of marriage if he didn't like kissing her. He hadn't hung around to find out what she thought.

She tossed and turned again. Then she closed her eyes and tried to think of other things. As the sun came up that morning, she finally drifted asleep.

Joe woke up early, immediately wondering if Anna had changed her mind. When he realized Julie really wanted him for a daddy, he thought he had a chance. But if Anna hated his kiss, there was no way. He couldn't agree to a sexless marriage. He wanted the whole enchilada, a real marriage, maybe even more children. Would she ever agree to something like that?

She certainly turned him on. He'd like to ask her

how his kiss had affected her. Maybe he'd visit her today, during naptime. He wanted to know her reaction. He got out of bed earlier than he usually did. He wasn't sure she even knew what real marriage was. He figured Derek hadn't done much to make her want romance.

Yeah, he'd definitely visit Anna today.

Joe knocked on her front door. He knew they were home because the rattletrap truck was parked out front. He knocked again, louder. He waited another two minutes, then he opened the door and stuck his head in.

"Anna?" Anna spun around and he realized she was holding Hank against her shoulder and the baby was crying. "What's going on? Is something wrong?"

"Hank's sick. He's running a high fever." Anna said, tears in her eyes.

"Have you called the doctor?"

She shook her head and turned her back on Joe as she patted her son's back.

Joe reached for the phone. Pete's doctor had become a friend and Joe dialed his number. The nurse informed him the doctor didn't have time for a friend's conversation. She'd tell the doctor to call him when he wasn't busy.

Before she could hang up, Joe ordered her to stop. "I'm calling about a patient. He's about nine months old. He's running a high fever and crying nonstop."

"Who is the patient?"

"Hank Pointer."

The nurse, sounding puzzled, asked, "Do you mean Henry Pointer? Doctor delivered him, but he's only seen him a couple of times since."

"Do you want to talk to his mother?"

"Yes, please."

Joe handed the phone to Anna and took Hank from his mom's arms.

Anna quietly talked into the phone.

Joe listened enough to hear Anna agree to take Hank into the doctor's office.

"I'll drive you. Where is Julie?"

"She's in bed sleeping."

He took the phone from her and called his mother. He quickly explained the situation to his mother and she promised to be there in five minutes.

"Mom's coming. She'll take Julie to her house once she wakes up. That way she'll get a good nap. She's not showing any symptoms, is she?"

"No. Not at all."

Joe continued to walk, holding the baby, telling her to go pack the diaper bag. She did as he said. Then she remembered to ask him why he was there. Joe didn't think honesty would be the best response. He told her he was there by coincidence. She nodded, distracted by Hank's screams. When his mother arrived, Joe led the way to his truck. Anna climbed in the truck and he handed her Hank after she fastened her seat belt. He drove carefully, but fast. When they came into the office, Hank woke all the other patients. The nurse asked them to follow her and she put the three of them in a private room.

"The doctor will be right with you."

Dr. Patrick Wilson came in, smiling and greeting Joe. He was a little more formal with Anna, "Mrs. Pointer, how are you?"

"I think she'll feel better when Hank feels better," Joe said.

"Right. Just put him on the table and let's have a look see. Has he been with other children lately?"

"He spent a day with Drew and Alexandra," Joe said.

"Damn! Alexandra came down with the measles yesterday. I would guess that's what is bothering Hank." A couple more minutes and the doctor said firmly. "Definitely the measles. Has Julie been vaccinated?"

"No, the doctor we were going to didn't think it was necessary at the time. Julie had already been exposed to it when she was younger," Anna said with a sigh. The doctor gave Hank some baby aspirin. It eased his crying. Patrick invited Anna to sit down and he talked about the care of the baby. He even told Anna it was a good thing, but Joe didn't believe it. He felt guilty.

"But it is especially good for boys. If he has it later, it can make him sterile," Patrick added.

With tears streaming down Anna's face, she gathered Hank's things and headed for the truck. Joe promised he'd get the prescriptions filled. While he was in the drugstore, he called his mother and told her what was wrong.

"Tell Anna she'd better bring them both here. It

will be too difficult to handle both of them by herself. And Joe, get extra amounts of the oatmeal bath.''

"I got one box," Joe replied.

"Get a couple more. It doesn't hurt them and it does make them feel better. Did you get calamine lotion?''

"Yes, Mom, the doctor recommended it. How's Julie?''

"Starting to feel some of the symptoms. I also called Kelly and she told me what the doctor had said, so I guessed what was happening.''

"All right. Do I need to bring anything with us?''

"Yes. Pick up some ice cream. It will make him feel better.''

"Okay. I'll be staying there too, if that's all right. I want to help.''

"Good, Julie will need a daddy. Temporarily of course.''

"Mom, don't tease like that in front of Anna. She gets upset.''

"Of course I won't do that. But I can't help thinking it would be a wonderful solution. Don't you?''

Joe gave her an indefinite answer and got off the phone. He was thinking about that. That was why he had come to see Anna today, to find out her reaction to his kiss. That was important, but he couldn't ask her now. She was completely occupied with Hank. She didn't even know yet that Julie was showing signs of succumbing, too. When she learned that she'd be doubly distracted. All he could do was support her until things were better.

At least, staying at his mother's with her, he'd bind

her closer to his family. Her children needed a big family. He thought about Julie. The child had taken to Drew. Drew liked her, too.

The best part of this fantasy would be when he could move them into his home and claim them for himself. It wasn't love. He was sure of that, wasn't he? He was attracted to her, of course, any man would be with her blond prettiness, her big blue eyes, her heart. She deserved the best.

He didn't think he was being egotistical to think he could provide for her and her children. He wasn't sure it would work out, but he wanted to try.

It would start with helping her get the kids well again. Then he'd figure out the best way to move in the right direction.

Chapter Seven

"We can't stay at your mother's house. What would people say?"

"Anna, what if Julie gets as sick as Hank? How will you manage?"

"I'll—I'll ask someone from the church to come help every once in a while."

"At two in the morning?"

"We'll manage. Joe, you're not going to have any reputation left if I take advantage of your mother."

"Who helped you when you had your babies?"

"Derek's mother helped a little when I had Julie. When Hank was born, I hired a lady friend of my mother-in-law to come in and take care of Julie."

"Family's better," he said calmly, sure he was right.

"Of course, family is better, but I didn't have any!"

His smile was satisfied which only irritated Anna more. "Was Julie doing all right?"

"She's already running a fever."

Anna moaned. Then her concern deepened. "What about Drew? The doctor said it was tough on little boys. Has he had measles?"

"Yeah, he had a mild case when he was smaller."

"Oh, good. So Kelly will only have one sick baby."

"Yeah." He parked his truck by the barn and hurried around the truck to help Anna out. "You carry Hank and I'll get everything else."

"I'm just going inside to thank Carol and collect Julie. I really can't stay here."

"Staying here will cause less gossip than it will if I come to your house."

She stared at him. "Are you threatening me?"

"No, sweetheart, but there's no way I'll leave you alone to take care of your kids with no help."

She sniffed and headed for the house. He followed along, adding more incentive.

"If you go off by yourself, mom will worry about you and try to come over, which will mess up Dad's life."

"I can manage."

"I'll watch you try to convince Mom of that." He knew she wouldn't. He was pretty sure his mother was trying to help him marry Anna, so she'd encourage Anna to stay no matter what.

As he'd predicted, Carol wouldn't hear of Anna going home with her kids alone. "Dear, there's no way

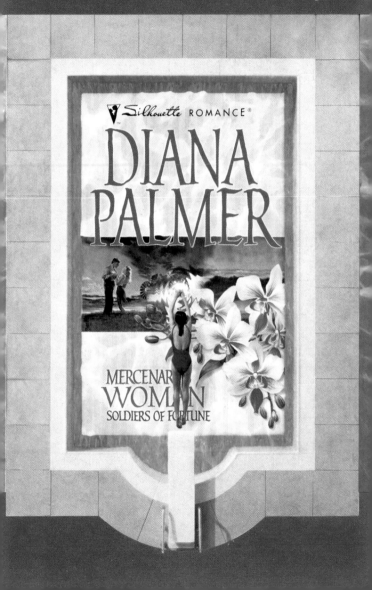

Silhouette ROMANCE®

DIANA PALMER

MERCENARY
WOMAN
SOLDIERS OF FORTUNE

We'd like to send you 2 FREE books and a surprise gift to introduce you to Silhouette Romance®. Accept our special offer today and

Get Ready for a totally Refreshing Experience!

HOW TO QUALIFY:

1. With a coin, carefully scratch off the silver area on the card at right to see what we have for you—2 FREE BOOKS and a FREE GIFT—ALL YOURS! ALL FREE!

2. Send back the card and you'll receive two brand-new Silhouette Romance® novels. These books have a cover price of $3.99 each in the U.S. and $4.50 each in Canada, but they are yours to keep absolutely free!

3. There's no catch. You're under no obligation to buy anything. We charge nothing— ZERO—for your first shipment and you don't have to make any minimum number of purchases—not even one!

4. The fact is, thousands of readers enjoy receiving books by mail from the Silhouette Reader Service™ Program. They enjoy the convenience of home delivery…they like getting the best new novels at discount prices, BEFORE they're available in stores…and they love their *Heart to Heart* subscriber newsletter featuring author news, horoscopes, recipes, book reviews and much more!

5. We hope that after receiving your free books you'll want to remain a subscriber. But the choice is yours—to continue or cancel, any time at all. So why not take us up on our invitation with no risk of any kind. You'll be glad you did!

SPECIAL FREE GIFT!

We can't tell you what it is…but we're sure you'll like it! A FREE gift just for giving the Silhouette Reader Service™ Program a try!

Visit us online at
www.eHarlequin.com

Your FREE Gifts include:
- 2 Silhouette Romance® books!
- An exciting mystery gift!

©2001 HARLEQUIN ENTERPRISES LTD. ® and TM are trademarks owned by Harlequin Books S.A. used under license.

Scratch off the silver area to see what the Silhouette Reader Service™ Program has for you.

Silhouette®
Where love comes alive®

YES!
I have scratched off the silver area above. Please send me the **2 FREE** books and gift for which I qualify. I understand I am under no obligation to purchase any books, as explained on the back and on the opposite page.

315 SDL DU3Z   215 SDL DU4H

FIRST NAME	LAST NAME

ADDRESS

APT.#	CITY

STATE/PROV.	ZIP/POSTAL CODE

(S-R-08/03)

they'll sleep the night through. You won't get any sleep at all.''

"I can manage," Anna said again, but Joe noticed her voice wasn't as strong as it had been earlier.

"I know you could, but it wouldn't be healthy. This way you'll have me to do the cooking and you can give the oatmeal baths. Joe can cover their bumps with calamine lotion and entertain when they aren't sleepy anymore. Measles are so irritating. Right, Joe?''

"Right, Mom. I remember when Michael had a bad case. I read so many books out loud to him, I could hardly talk.'' He smiled at Anna.

"But Mr. Crawford won't like his schedule being messed up,'' Anna said, desperately scrambling for reasons to go home. He didn't think she'd use the real reasons, that she was trying to avoid talk.

When she couldn't come up with another reason, Carol nodded. "Good. That's settled.''

Anna started to say something else, but Carol had an idea. "Why don't you run to your house and bring some clothes for all of you? Julie is still asleep and it looks like poor little Hank has worn himself out with his crying.''

Joe took Anna's arm and began moving toward the door. "Good idea, Mom.''

"Wait!'' Anna protested.

"Now, Anna, I don't mind if you nurse your children naked, but people might talk about such loose behavior,'' Joe teased.

She glared at him, but she didn't try to pull away.

In the truck, she remained silent, staring straight ahead.

"If you're worried about me taking advantage of our situation, just tell me when I make you uncomfortable."

She said nothing.

"I mean, sometimes kisses are a good thing."

Silence.

Changing to a pitiful voice, he said, "Did you hate it that much?"

"No!" she exclaimed. Then she clamped her lips together and refused to look at him. Joe's spirits rose. She hadn't hated his kiss. He was anxious to kiss her again.

Anna hurriedly packed the only suitcase she owned, taking most of the room for her two children. She couldn't turn down the help being offered. She knew the kids would be happy being spoiled by the Crawfords.

But she had to avoid Joe.

She hadn't meant to sound like she enjoyed his kiss, but he'd sounded so pitiful. She figured he'd been pretending, but she'd fallen for his playacting.

The next few days were going to be a test and she had to remain strong.

"I'm ready," she said quietly as she came into the living room where she'd told Joe to wait.

"That was fast."

"I'm afraid the children might wake up and I want to be there."

"Good idea. We'll hurry."

He talked about the crops and the baby calves he'd had recently. Anything to take her mind off her sick children. She said nothing, but she didn't cry.

When he pulled to a stop, he told her to go on in and he'd bring her suitcase. She hurried into the house.

That afternoon, Joe tried to make himself useful. Anna was such a good mother, spending every minute with her children. Hank was beginning to break out. Julie wasn't so lucky. Her fever was running high and she was uncomfortable. Anna held her and rocked her, singing soft little songs.

When his mother told them dinner was ready, Anna refused to leave Julie.

"Of course not, child. Caleb and I will hold the children and try to get them to eat. You and Joe need to keep your strength up."

"Oh, no! I couldn't ask you to—"

"You're not asking, child. We're volunteering. And don't forget we saw six children through these illnesses."

"Of course, but I don't think it's right for you to—"

Carol took Julie from her mother and whispered into the little girl's ear. Julie nodded and settled her head on Carol's shoulder.

Joe told his mother he'd bring Hank.

"Thank you, dear."

He shifted Hank to one shoulder and grabbed Anna's arm, pulling her along with him.

"Joe," she whispered. I really can't let them—"

"Dad is going to be real upset that you don't think him able to hold old Hank here. He's good at rocking little boys. Lots of practice."

"Joe, you know that's not the reason. I'm sure he'd be very good, but he shouldn't have to use his dinnertime to take care of my kids."

Joe's only response was what he'd been wanting to do all day. He bent down and kissed her again.

He withdrew slowly and she didn't pull away. "Ask him, sweetheart. He'll tell you it makes him feel young again. He loves little kids."

Inside, he was celebrating. She hadn't even told him not to kiss her. He escorted her into the kitchen before she could say anything.

While Anna explained that she'd manage so the Crawfords could have a quiet dinner, Joe settled across from his parents, saving the other place for Anna.

"Oh, I didn't explain," Carol said. "We had our quiet dinner first. Now it's your time. We used to eat in shifts all the time. It's normal to eat in shifts."

"But—"

"Give me the baby, son. I'm best with little boys. I like little girls but they can fool me."

Carol laughed. "He's an old softy. Lindsay used to get her way all the time. I'd have to step in because she was getting completely spoiled." She turned to Joe. "Now fill her plate for her, Joe. I'd bet she didn't eat lunch."

Anna blinked in surprise. Lunch? She couldn't remember. Suddenly her stomach growled and her cheeks turned red.

"Don't apologize, child. I knew you were one of those mothers who don't think of themselves when their children were in need. That's the way it should be, but now you have to catch up so you can keep going."

She was hungry. She ate so much she was embarrassed. When she'd finished, Joe's mother set a bowl of ice cream in front of Anna.

"Oh, no, I couldn't—"

"I figured you'd say that, but Julie will like it. It will cool down her throat."

"Oh, of course."

The peaceful meal was as helpful to Anna as the calamine lotion was to Julie. Though she was tired when she rose from the table, she thought she could make it through the evening. She would need to give them the oatmeal baths. Julie only had a couple of bumps, but Hank was covered. Joe had spent all afternoon with him. He was good with Hank…Henry. She was losing her distance.

On the third day, Hank took his regular nap while Julie tossed and turned and asked her mother to make it stop itching.

"Do you think Hank is better, or worse?" she asked Carol. She'd come to depend on the woman a lot.

Carol slid her arm around Anna's slumping shoulders. "I think he's getting well."

Anna's relief caused her to do the one thing she'd tried to avoid. Her head fell on Carol's shoulder and tears ran down her cheek. "Oh, thank God."

"Now don't think that means he's completely recovered. He's lost some stamina and weight. You'll have to bring him back slowly."

"Hey! What's going on? I leave you alone for five minutes and you start crying?" Joe said from the doorway.

Anna swung away from his gaze and hurriedly wiped her cheeks. "N-nothing!"

"Nonsense. We think Hank is getting well. And we think it won't be long before Julie follows," Carol told Joe.

"Oh, thank you, Carol. Your help has been wonderful."

"What about me? I worked, too. Don't I get a thank-you?"

After a hesitation, she reached out to give him a hug. But she knew what was going to come. Joe had begun to spread his kisses around whenever he thought she needed a lift. Sure enough, his lips covered hers and he tugged her close.

"Joe!" She pulled away. "What will your mother think?"

"She was headed to the door before I touched you. She has great discretion."

"Oh, no, I'm afraid she'll be upset!"

Joe kissed her again, a quick sassy kiss that almost made her smile.

"She's probably got her fingers crossed that you'll be so grateful, you'll marry me!"

She blushed and moved away from him. She didn't want to discuss this now. She had to turn him down.

Otherwise she'd be taking advantage of him. There were minutes when he was so tempting with his smiles, his kisses, his strength, that she was having difficulty resisting. But Carol's conclusion that both children were on the mend meant she wouldn't have to stay here much longer. That was good news.

Three days later she knew she'd made a mistake. Being away from Joe didn't solve all her problems.

Julie came running into the kitchen and Anna knew she was about to hear her question again.

"Mommy, when is Joe coming to see us?"

"I don't know, Julie. I'm sure he has a lot of work to do since he didn't work on his farm while you were sick."

"But we haven't seen him in three days!" Julie exclaimed.

Anna was unhappy that Julie had learned how to count.

"Did you pick up your toys like I asked?"

Julie pouted. "I want Joe to see my coloring. He'll like it."

"True, but I'm going to be unhappy if he comes to see us and the house is dirty."

Julie stuck her finger in her mouth, in deep thought. Finally she started for her bedroom.

"Where are you going?" Anna asked.

"I'm going to clean up my room so Joe will come."

"Good." Anna wasn't sure how she would explain why Joe didn't visit when Julie's room was clean. Julie seemed so sure Joe would visit them.

She wasn't. She believed that Joe had realized she wouldn't marry him. That would keep him away. When she opened the weekly newspaper from Lawton the next morning her jaw dropped and her mouth hung open. The top of the first page had a big picture of Joe with his arms around a blond young woman staring up at him with adoration in her gaze.

"Julie, look. Here's a picture of Joe."

Julie hopped down from her chair and ran to her mommy's side. "That's Joe!" she exclaimed. Then her smile disappeared. "Who is she?" Julie asked, pointing out the young woman.

"I don't know, sweetie. She looks like a friend of Joe's."

"I don't like her!"

"She looks very nice," Anna assured her daughter. She understood Julie's feelings, but she had to make Julie realize that she had to give up her hope of having Joe as her father.

Julie stared at the picture again. "I don't like her," Julie repeated. Then after several moments of silence, Julie looked at Anna. "Joe's not really going to be my daddy, is he?"

"No, honey, he's not. He'll marry a nice lady, like this one, and have his own children."

Julie looked stricken. Tears filled her eyes and she walked slowly out of the room. Anna wanted to cuddle her and tell her she'd find her a daddy, but she wouldn't lie to her daughter.

The sound of a truck stopping in her front yard brought Anna to the front window. A red truck had parked and she watched with a quick flutter of her heart as Joe headed for her front door.

When he knocked on the door, she slowly opened it. "Hi, Joe. Is something wrong?"

"Not if you all are all right."

"Of course we are." When Joe just stood there, she reluctantly took a step back. "Do you want come in?"

"Of course I do. I'm under strict instructions to check out the kids. And to give them these cookies from mom."

"Oh, your mother shouldn't have gone to so much trouble."

"She loves to bake cookies. Besides, she wanted the kids to know she hasn't forgotten them."

"No, of course not. Julie and I wrote a thank-you note for Carol yesterday. She should get it tomorrow."

"Good. She'll like that. Did you write me a thank-you note?"

"Of course we did," Anna said, not looking at him. He wouldn't be pleased with the formal tones and she knew it.

He must have figured that out. He put his hands on her shoulders and turned her around. "Why won't I like it?"

"I didn't say you wouldn't."

He gave her a wry smile. "Somehow I figured it out from the expression on your face."

Anna heard little footsteps coming down the hall. "I'll tell the children your mother sent the cookies."

"You're ready for me to leave?" he asked, staring at Anna.

"I don't want to wake the children and have them get overexcited."

"They're already in bed?"

"Yes. They're still recovering."

"Mom thought they'd be all recovered. I'd better look at them. She's going to be worried."

He started around Anna and she grabbed his arm. "No! They—"

"Joe!" Julie exclaimed. "It is you!"

"Of course it is, my angel. How are you?"

"I was doing okay until I saw that picture…"

Anna closed her eyes so Joe couldn't see how upset she was.

Joe squatted down to Julie's level. "What picture, Julie?"

"The picture in the paper where you're hugging that girl."

Joe stood and looked at Anna. "What's she talking about?" he asked.

Anna flipped over the newspaper and slid it across the table. She turned away, hoping she could hide her anguish.

"Are you talking about this girl?"

"Yes!" Julie exclaimed. "You like her better than me."

"I do not. That was a posed picture."

"What's that mean?" Julie demanded.

"It means they asked us to hug each other."

"Why?" Julie demanded.

"Julie, that's none of your business," Anna interrupted.

"Sure it is. I had to hug her because I saved her life last year."

"You did? How?" Julie asked again, not at all deterred by her mother's orders.

"She was swimming and got the cramps. I was volunteering as a lifeguard and saw her go under. I swam out and saved her. They wanted to remind people that it happened so they give more money to the community programs."

"So you don't love her more than us?" Julie asked eagerly.

"Of course not. In fact, I want to marry your mommy and be your daddy. Didn't she tell you?"

Chapter Eight

Julie screamed and threw herself into Joe's waiting arms.

"No!" Anna said loudly, trying to halt the ridiculous celebration. However much she was attracted to Joe, she knew she wasn't the right woman for him. She wasn't going to trap him into marriage.

Julie appeared on the edge of tears. "Mommy, Joe wants to be my daddy! Why do you say no?"

"Because we can't take advantage of Joe. We can't marry him." Anna drew a deep breath, trying to hide her shaking fingers.

Joe lowered Julie to the floor. "Go read a storybook, sweetheart, and let me talk to your mother. I'll convince her."

"Okay, but try real hard, Joe."

He kissed her cheek and turned her in the direction of the door. "I will. Now scoot."

Anna wanted to keep Julie beside her. She needed her presence to keep from giving in to Joe's suggestion. She closed her eyes and prayed for strength. When he touched her shoulders, she stiffened and opened her eyes. "Joe, you shouldn't have told Julie that. You know you should find a woman to marry who doesn't already have children."

"Why? Do you think I'm too young to be Julie's daddy?"

"No, of course not, but you deserve someone to have *your* children."

"Are you telling me you can't have more children? Or won't have *my* children?"

She clamped her lips together, trying to keep the words in. Of course she wanted to have his children. After Derek's indifference to their children, Joe's enthusiasm would be a delight. "That's not the point, Joe. You should have your first child with someone who would share her first time with you."

"Why take on someone inexperienced when I can have someone who has proven she has wonderful children?"

"Joe, you're being ridiculous!"

He caught her shoulders and pulled her to him. When his lips covered hers, she melted. His kisses were so sweet.

He leaned back. "See, you like kissing me."

"Joe, there's more to marriage than being a good kisser. Derek was a good kisser!"

His eyes narrowed. "I can kiss better than him."

"How do you know?" After swallowing, she said, "It doesn't matter."

"You're right, because you owe me," Joe teased.

"How do you figure that?"

"I've helped you with your problems."

"Yes, you did, but *you* decided to do all that. I didn't ask you to help me."

"That's true. But I need to marry you so I can get married again."

She stared at him in surprise. "I beg your pardon?"

"I've noticed that a lot of women are flirting with me since I've showed up with you. And I've asked some of the guys who've been divorced. They say the women are all over them. Seems women want what they can't have."

"And you expect me to marry you so you can divorce me? That's stupid! Think what that would do to Julie? She'd think you were her daddy and she finds you flirting with other women? And then you leave us? I can't believe you'd be so cruel."

His face showed chagrin, as if he were surprised by the failure of his plan. "Well, that didn't work very well, did it?"

"No, it didn't. I don't know why you would even suggest such a thing. It would be terrible for Julie."

"How about I promise you twenty years?"

"What are you talking about? Twenty years of what?"

He stepped closer again. "Twenty years of marriage. I won't leave you for the first twenty years."

"Joe, that's crazy. What if you're miserable those twenty years? And when you divorced me, you'd be fifty-five. It would be too late for you to marry again and have more children."

"Okay, here's the truth. I don't seem to have luck where women are concerned—I never thought I'd get married. If I marry you, I'll have two children at once and maybe another one or two...before it's too late. I want to be a father."

Anna stared at him. "What are you saying? How can you have trouble with women?"

"Well," he said, "I'm not the most attractive man around, and my size seems to intimidate women. Most ladies around these parts would be disappointed with me. But you're not interested in a love match. And I can provide for your children and any others we might have. It's a perfect plan."

"Joe, that's an absurd plan. I'm sure you can find someone else."

"And I'm sure I can't. We can give it a try and if it doesn't work, you can divorce me at any time. I'll set up trust funds for the children that will take care of their future. They could have security."

Anna turned away from him, hoping he wouldn't see the desire to say yes. She was trying to save him from himself.

"Joe, this is crazy."

"Julie and I don't think so."

"I can't do this. Any woman would tell you it's ridiculous."

"So ask a woman. Then tell me what she says."

"I don't know anyone who isn't connected to you!"

"Let's go back to Mom's. I won't say anything to her. You can talk to her while I show the kids some animals in the barn. She'll give you her honest opinion."

"Joe, I...and you'll agree with what she says?"

She watched Joe's face, looking for an indication that he was being careful.

He hesitated. Then he said, "Yes, I will."

With a sigh, Anna nodded. She was pretty sure his mother wouldn't go along with his plan.

"I will as long as you're honest with her."

She jerked her head up. "What?"

"As long as you answer any of her questions honestly."

"Well, of course."

He smiled at her, then said he'd get the kids.

"But what are we going to tell Julie?" Anna asked.

"I'll take care of it. She won't pester you," Joe promised. Before she could protest, he had disappeared.

Joe didn't know how determined Julie could be, Anna thought. That's why she had to end everything here and now. Otherwise the child could drive her crazy.

Joe had his fingers crossed on the steering wheel of his big truck. He'd spent the last two days in almost continuous discussions with his parents. He'd explained to them how he felt about Anna. And he'd asked for their help and advice about explaining to

Anna and convincing her to marry him. His idea had failed. Now, he was depending on his mother. He knew his mother liked Anna. She'd been impressed with how dedicated Anna was to her children.

Even more, she swore she thought Anna loved him. She said she'd seen Anna staring after him when she didn't think anyone saw her. Joe prayed his mother was right. It would at least mean she was interested. That was progress.

When the four of them entered his mother's kitchen, Joe said, "Mom, I'm going to take the kids to the barn to see the animals. Would you fix some lemonade to go with the cookies you sent to the children?"

"Of course I can. I wanted to see the kids, but I didn't want to intrude," Carol said with her big grin. Julie pleased her by thanking her for the cookies and the lemonade in advance. After Joe took the children away, she smiled at Anna. "Your daughter didn't get her manners from her father. You've done a nice job raising them, Anna."

"Thank you, Carol, and thank you for the cookies. Julie was feeling a little lonely. The cookies cheered her right up."

"I imagine Joe cheered her up more. She seems very fond of him."

That was a perfect lead-in. She wet her suddenly dry lips and hesitated before she said, "Carol, I need to talk to you."

"Why, of course," Carol said with that big smile of hers. Anna thought she was the nicest person in the whole world.

"I—need some advice and I don't know too many people I can ask."

"Giving advice is my specialty. I usually give it whether they ask for it or not!" she said with a chuckle. "What is it?"

"Joe asked me to marry him." When Carol beamed at her, she held up a hand. "No, wait. I think he asked because he loves Julie and, I suppose Hank. He seems to worry about having a family life with someone who—who doesn't have experience parenting. I've tried to explain to him that he should experience it with a woman he loves, but—I'm not making a lot of progress. What do you think?" She twisted her hands together, watching Carol closely.

"So, he didn't say he loves you?"

"No, of course not. I wouldn't expect that. I understand that it is my children who draw him. I'm fortunate he feels that way. It would be a major concern if I were to agree to marry him."

"I see. How do you feel about my son?"

Uh-oh. Now is when that promise to be honest comes into play, she realized. She stared at her hands. "Your son is a wonderful man. He's gentle, loving and kind."

"Yes, he is."

"I can't believe he can't find anyone to marry."

Carol turned her back on Anna. "I used to think that, too. But now I realize he was waiting for someone special to come along."

Anna jerked her head up, staring at Carol. "You think he's found someone...I mean, who is it?"

"I think it's you, Anna."

Anna began backing away. "Oh, no, it's not me. He loves my kids."

"Well, let's try this one more time. Do you love Joe?"

"Yes, I do, but I don't want him to have second-best. He doesn't deserve that."

"Any man who receives a woman's true love in return for marriage is lucky."

"No, I'm not like the women in your family who do everything so well and help their husbands. I couldn't even take care of my children until Joe came along."

Carol stepped across the room and hugged Anna. "But you kept trying, Anna. You had a lot of choices, but you put your children before yourself and kept working. My advice is to marry him. I think you'll put him first, too. He can't ask for more than that." With another hug, Carol began pouring lemonade in glasses for all of them. Automatically Anna began taking them to the table. Carol smiled. Anna was an automatic helper, and she thought she would make Joe very happy.

When Joe and the children came back from the barn, Hank had nothing to say except in slobbers. He was cutting a tooth, but he nestled in Joe's arm, content. It was obvious Julie had been warned not to say anything. But she kept staring at her mother, waiting for her to say something important.

"Drink your lemonade," Anna said, composed now

that she'd made her decision with Carol's approval. "I'm going to talk to Joe for a few minutes."

She got up and left the room, not looking to see if Joe followed. Either he did or he didn't. If he didn't, she wouldn't have to make a decision.

Joe, of course, was on her heels as she reached the family room. He took her by the shoulders and turned her around, holding her against him. "You've made your decision?" he asked.

"Joe, are you sure?"

"That I want to marry you?" He pulled her into his arms and kissed her again. But this time, he put himself into the kiss, and Anna stepped back from his arms to stare at him in shock. His kisses had been sweet, gentle. That kiss had felt hungry.

"Does that tell you?" he asked with a grin. "You've truly agreed to marry me, for us to become a family?"

"Yes."

He swooped down on her and swung her around. "Come on, let's go tell Julie and Hank."

In no time, Julie was laughing and cheering. She and Joe were dancing around the kitchen. Anna sat in one of the chairs, holding Hank who kept reaching for Joe when he got close to Anna's chair.

"When will we get married?" Julie asked when she'd settled down a little.

"I don't know," Anna said. "We'll set a time later," she assured her child.

"No!" Joe exploded. "We need to get married at once. I'm too old to wait. I have no time to wait."

"No time to wait...for what?" Anna asked, confused.

"For the good part of my life. How about Sunday?"

Anna nodded slowly. "Sunday is always a nice day for a wedding. We'll have to see when the pastor is free. Or he might prefer not to have a wedding on Sunday because he has two sessions, you know. Are we asking Pastor White to perform the ceremony?"

"If it's okay with you," Joe said, leaning over to kiss her again, one of those sweet kisses rather than a hungry one. "I've already checked with him. He's free Sunday."

Anna's eyes opened wider. "You don't mean this Sunday?"

"Yes, of course. There's no reason to wait, is there?"

"But I have nothing to wear. If I had time, I could make something for all three of us and save some money."

Joe pulled her into his arms. "I'm sure what you would make would be beautiful. But I don't want to wait for my family. Mother can take you shopping tomorrow and buy you something to wear. Right, Mom?"

"Of course, dear. Lindsay and Kelly just got a new shipment in. But only if Anna is in agreement."

Anna sat there in shock, as if suddenly she didn't know what was happening. She'd agreed to marry Joe, thinking they'd be engaged for a couple of months at least and she could think about it. Now she'd agreed to be married in four days. Her life was suddenly going to change. She'd made this decision, but she wasn't sure she was prepared for the consequences.

Anna insisted Joe take them back home for dinner. She even invited him to stay and eat. That was more than he'd expected. He saw hesitation in her eyes and that worried him. That hesitation was the reason for his forcing a quick marriage. It was true he didn't want to wait, but the most important reason was to not give Anna time to change her mind.

"What are we having for dinner?" he asked as they drove home.

"I was going to make macaroni and cheese for dinner for the children and add a salad, but I guess you need more than that." She sounded worried.

Joe grinned. "Honey, I could eat all that or nothing and be perfectly happy. You're going to marry me, that's all that matters. Right, Julie?"

"That's right, Joe! You're going to be my daddy. That's what's important."

"Thanks, Julie. I hope Hank likes the idea as well as you do."

"He will," Julie said with such assurance even her mother laughed.

"Well, it's nice to know that everyone's happy," Anna said.

Joe thought she sounded just a little put out. He parked in front of her porch and then got out and came around to help Julie out and pick up Hank's carrier. As Anna slid down from the high truck seat, he leaned against her warm body. "Are you happy about it?" he whispered.

Anna kept her eyes low. "Of course I am, Joe," she said.

"I don't see you dancing around like Julie is."

"I've been married before, Joe."

"Our marriage won't be like yours with Derek. I can promise you that, Anna."

Anna looked up into his eyes and said nothing. He wanted to sweep her off her feet and carry her into the house, but he waited.

Finally, she smiled a cautious smile and said, "Thanks." Then she slipped away from him and ran into the house.

He followed her. He had no intention of giving up an evening spent with his soon-to-be family. After putting Hank down on the sofa in his carrier, he looked at Anna hustling around the kitchen. "What can I do to help?" he asked.

The look she gave him had a sparkle of amusement. "Are you serious?" she asked.

"Of course I am."

"Well, what would be the most help would be to change Hank's diaper and go ahead and give him his bath. Then after he eats, he can go right to bed."

Joe saw the challenge in her eyes. Aha, she was giving him a test. "No problem," he said with a smile. "Come on, Hank ole boy. Let's show Mommy how good we are."

"I'll help," Julie announced.

"No, Julie. I need you to set the table," Anna said, stopping her child's exit.

"But, Mommy!"

"Sorry, sweetie. Put the silverware and plates on the table please." She kept Julie in the kitchen with her.

Joe was sure it was part of the test. He couldn't get any help from Julie about where everything was located. But half an hour later, he and Hank returned. The baby was shiny clean and happy as could be. Hank loved baths. Joe, on the other hand, looked a little worse for wear. Hank had delighted in splashing him. But he had accomplished his job. He held Hank out and gave an exclamatory, "Ta-da!"

Anna calmly nodded in his direction. "I see you found his pajamas."

"Yes, I did. I passed the test."

Anna's eyes rounded in mock innocence. "I don't know what you're talking about. Hank takes his bath every night."

"Well, now you know I'm capable of helping."

"Yes, and I appreciate it. Put him in his high chair and pull him to the table. Julie, get the bib for Hank."

Joe let Julie tie Hank's bib on and the baby immediately started trying to pull it off. "Whoa, son. Let's keep the bib on," he suggested.

Anna set some jars of baby food on the table. "If you'll start feeding him, he'll forget about the bib."

He discovered she was right. He stuffed Hank's mouth full of baby food and teased Julie until Anna began setting dinner on the table. They were still having macaroni and cheese and salad, but she'd added chicken, cheese, raw broccoli and bacon to the salad. Joe had expected to go home hungry, but he found the salad satisfying. Especially when he ate the macaroni and cheese, too.

He'd gotten so enthused about the meal, he looked over at Hank and found him slumped over, asleep. Anna came around the table.

"I'll take him to bed."

"Sure you don't want me to do it?" Joe asked. "It could be part of the test."

This time Anna's cheeks flushed. "I told you there was no test, Joe. You're being ridiculous."

He caught her hand and pulled her onto his knee. After giving her a smacking kiss he said, "Doesn't matter, as long as I passed."

She got up from his lap, kissed him on the cheek and said, "You did," and then carried Hank away.

When she'd left the room he looked at Julie. She was pretty sleepy, too. "Are you ready for bed, too, Julie?"

"No!" the child protested, even as her eyes closed.

Anna came in and took Julie away. Joe cleaned the table and realized for the first time that Anna didn't have a dishwasher. He ran the sink full of hot water, added soap, and began washing the dishes.

"Joe! You don't need to do the dishes," Anna said. "I'll do them."

"But you did the cooking. It's only fair that I clean up. It was a great meal."

"Go on home, I'll finish it."

Joe took his hands out of the water and dried them. "You're just trying to get rid of me."

"Well, I'll admit, I'm a little tired."

He pulled her to him and kissed her before he turned to the door. "Only three more days, Anna. Then we'll be together."

He left, and Anna stood there, still finding it hard to believe she'd agreed to marry him on Sunday.

Chapter Nine

When Anna met Carol at her house the next morning, Joe was there to baby-sit.

"Are you sure you want to baby-sit? Don't you need to work?" Anna asked.

Joe grinned. "Worried about how I'll pay the bills already?"

"No, of course not," Anna assured him, embarrassed.

"Joe," his mother interrupted. "Quit embarrassing your bride. The sandwiches are already made in the refrigerator for lunch. We're going to eat with Lindsay and Kelly."

That thought pleased Anna, but she worried she was causing too much trouble.

As if reading her mind, Carol smiled and said, "They're looking forward to it."

Anna believed Carol when she entered the store. Both ladies met her with a hug.

"Congratulations!" They exclaimed together.

"Oh, no!" Lindsay said. "That's what we're supposed to tell Joe. We'll just welcome you to the family, Anna."

"Yes, you're going to be a great addition," Kelly said. "We need more women in this family."

"We've picked out the perfect dress and saved it in your size. You're going to love it!" Lindsay exclaimed.

In no time they had Anna and Carol sitting in chairs as if they were in a very expensive shop, showing them Anna's choices. And in the end, they were right. The dress they'd chosen was a soft pink. It fit Anna's small waist and flared out around her legs. The sleeves were full with long cuffs. And its soft color matched the color of her cheeks.

"Oh, it's beautiful!" Anna said with a gasp.

"Isn't it?" Lindsay agreed. "And here's the one we thought would match it for Julie."

She showed Anna a small dress the same color as the first, almost made alike. The only differences were some embroidered blue flowers and a high waistline.

Anna laughed. "I can explain to Julie that she has flowers on her dress because she's the flower girl." They all chuckled.

"We didn't know what to do about Hank. I assume you don't want to dress him in pink?" Kelly teased.

"Heavens, no!" Anna exclaimed. "Joe has already

chastised me for calling him Henry. Do you have something in blue?''

The ladies found a knit suit for the baby in royal blue, and they were done.

''Well,'' Carol said. ''We're all finished. Ready to go to lunch?''

Kelly checked her watch and nodded. ''Good, that will give us lots of time to talk.''

They went to the pizza place across the street. Carol excused herself. Anna took the opportunity to talk to her future sisters-in-law alone.

''I'm not sure I'm doing the right thing.''

Lindsay frowned. ''What do you mean? Don't you love Joe?''

''Of course I do. But he just loves my children.''

Kelly stared at her. ''Did he tell you that?'' she asked, scandalized.

''Not exactly. But it's all he talks about.''

Lindsay stared at Anna, tapping her finger on the table while she thought. ''I think it's because Joe's shy. He never dated much in high school. Maybe he needs someone to, you know, talk to him.''

Kelly and Anna both stared at her until Anna asked the obvious question. ''You mean about sex?'' She remembered that kiss he'd given her and had her doubts about that need.

''But who do you intend to…'' Kelly began. ''Oh no.'' She'd just realized Lindsay was looking intently at her. ''You want me to ask Pete to talk to Joe about marriage?''

"Well, I think it would come better from his own brother than his brother-in-law."

"Okay, okay. I'll do it," Kelly said.

Before Anna could say anything else, Carol rejoined them pulling several sheets of paper from her purse.

"I organized a few things last night and I've divided them up. We'll have the shower tomorrow in place of a bride's party. Joe will have the men to deal with, so he'll be busy."

"A shower," Anna protested. "No, that won't be necessary. I hardly know anyone."

"I know, dear," Carol said, patting her hand. "But Joe has lived here all his life. He has lots of friends who want to help celebrate his wedding."

Carol continued through her notes. "Kelly and Lindsay, we're going to have a slumber party for all the grandchildren on Sunday night. Family tradition."

Lindsay spoke up. "I don't remember that tradition."

"We're just starting it," Carol explained calmly. "Otherwise Julie will expect to go on the honeymoon with her new dad and mom. She'll enjoy having Drew there, and Hank and Alexandra get along well."

"Do you want me to keep them, Mom?" Lindsay offered.

"No, thank you. That will be the fun part of the evening. Kelly, I'll call your mom later today, but do you think she can do the wedding cake?"

"Of course she can," said Kelly.

"Dear, are your shoes comfortable?" asked Carol. "The reception line is going to be long."

"Yes," Lindsay agreed. "And if you grow faint, the rumors will immediately begin that you're pregnant. That happened to me."

"Well, they only missed by a couple of days," Kelly pointed out, grinning.

"You don't have room to talk," Lindsay teased back.

Anna watched the two women, enjoying their friendship. She hoped Julie would grow up with good friends. They were certainly going to become a part of the community. She was giving her two children a wonderful gift: A family. Suddenly she felt better about what she'd agreed to do.

"Hello?" Pete said, grabbing the phone in his barn.

"Pete, it's me."

"Hello, sweetheart. You coming home early? I've missed you today."

"No. In fact, I might be a little late. I'm stopping by my mother's house to figure out what kind of wedding cake to make for Joe."

"Lordy mercy, Mom's got out those pieces of paper."

Kelly didn't need to ask what he meant. Carol got so much accomplished because she planned carefully. And that included the people who would be drafted.

"Mmm, I'm afraid so. Are you going to be involved in Joe's bachelor party?"

"I suppose, but she hasn't called me yet," Pete said as he swung another bale of hay into place, the phone tucked behind his ear. His wife said something but he didn't understand her hurriedly muttered words. "What was that?" he asked.

"You didn't hear me?"

"No. Try me again."

"Okay. Um, are you going to have a talk with Joe?"

Pete shifted another bale of hay while he thought about what his wife had said. "You mean about what to do for the bachelor party?"

"No."

"Then what would I have a talk about?"

"Sex."

Pete was stunned. Then he fell to the floor in laughter. His friend's partner and Kelly's stepfather, Rafe, stared at Pete. He'd come over to discuss some work for the next day. "Are you okay, boy?"

"Yeah. Wait until I tell you." He picked up the phone again. "Kelly, we'll discuss this when you get home." Then he explained Kelly's request. Rafe too joined in the laughter. Until he said, "You going to do it?"

"Naw! I can't. Joe explained everything to me. Just because he hasn't married doesn't mean he doesn't know anything. He'd be insulted. I don't know what Kelly has in her head, but I don't think Joe needs a sex talk! He must not be communicating well!"

They'd gone into the kitchen for a cup of coffee before Rafe started back to Gil's ranch, when the phone rang again.

This time it was Gil Daniels, Lindsay's husband. "You lookin' for me?" Rafe asked.

"No. But I don't know what to tell Lindsay. She's expecting someone to explain things to Joe."

"Things?" Rafe asked, even though he knew what Gil was saying. "Have the girls elected you to have the talk?"

Pete, listening in, just shook his head. He took the phone away from Rafe. "Joe gave me the talk. He doesn't need one."

"Good. You tell Lindsay that!"

"Damn! I'd rather tell Joe than Lindsay."

"I know. She'll want to ask questions!"

"How about all of us talk to him together?" Rafe said. "You know how persistent these women are."

"That's a good idea," Pete said. "Come on over here, Gil. We'll invite Joe over."

"I'm not sure this will work."

"It will," Pete assured his brother-in-law.

When Joe drove up in his brother's barnyard, he noticed Rafe's pickup and also Gil Daniels'. What was going on?

In the barn, the three men were sitting on some barrels in a circle. There was an empty one, so Joe joined them. "Howdy, boys."

Pete jumped up, as if he was nervous. "Joe, you're here!"

"Yeah. You called me."

"Yeah. That's because our wives called us."

"Really? Is something up?"

Rafe chuckled, but he looked away when Joe stared

at him. "My wife knew better than to call," he muttered.

Gil stirred on his barrel. "I didn't know what to do."

"About what?" Joe asked.

"I told them it wasn't necessary," Pete said. "But in a way it is. Kelly had a previous husband, like Anna."

Joe stared at each one of them. "You're offering to give me a facts-of-life talk?" he asked in disbelief.

"I told them you gave me mine when I was sixteen, but the girls…well, we didn't know what to tell them. Now we can say yes, we did."

"I see."

"I can tell you that Kelly was slow to relax. What I heard about that jerk explains it. Has Anna talked much about Derek?"

Joe shook his head in response.

"You got any questions?" Gil asked.

"Yeah, I'd really like that recipe Lindsay uses for corn bread." He grinned at the other men.

They all protested, but he assured them he knew how to be patient and gentle.

Then he suggested they play cards, since they weren't getting any work done.

Anna found the time to have a long talk with Julie. The child figured out right away that the slumber party was because she wasn't going with Joe and her mom. "Why? Where are you going?"

"We're just going to Joe's house so we can get used to living together."

"I can help. Joe likes me."

"Yes, he does, sweetheart, but things are going to change now. For example, you can't run out of the bathroom with no clothes on."

"Why?" Julie asked, a puzzled look on her face.

"You know boys are different from girls."

"Yes."

"Well, boys and girls aren't supposed to appear naked in front of each other unless they're married." Anna thought she'd explained that very well. But Julie took no time to show her she hadn't.

"But Mommy, that's not a problem. We're going to be married!" she explained, smiling at Anna.

"Um, Julie, Joe and I are going to be married. You aren't going to be married to Joe. Just like you aren't married to Hank. When he gets older, you won't share a bath with him like you do now occasionally."

"You mean I get shut out? I'm all alone?"

"Only when you're naked. Until you get married. Then you can—can do things together, but getting married is a serious thing."

Julie crossed her arms across her chest. "I don't like this!"

"I know, dear, but you'll still have lots of fun. We do everything together and we're not naked."

"So I can't come into your bedroom unless you say it's okay? Otherwise you're going to be naked?"

Anna struggled with the image of what Julie had described. She had hidden from the thought of intimacy with Joe. "Uh, not necessarily, but everyone needs some privacy. That's why I always knock on your door before I enter it." She was glad she had something else for Julie to focus on besides being naked.

"I think I should talk to Joe about this!" Julie said, jumping to her feet.

"No!"

"Why not?" Julie demanded suspiciously.

"Because it will—embarrass me."

"*I* won't be embarrassed!" Julie exclaimed and stalked out of the room.

"I'm sure you won't," Anna said with a sigh.

Joe was to pick them up that evening to take them to the shower. Not only did Anna have to worry about her own jitters, she was also worried about Julie. She'd been very quiet as she'd done their hair and put on a second new dress bought exclusively for the shower.

"Do you like your new dress?" she asked in a cheerful voice.

"Yes, thank you."

"I think it looks very pretty on you."

"Thank you."

Good manners. That was a good sign.

"Is Drew going to be there?" Julie asked.

"Mmm, no. I don't think so. I think he'll stay with his father."

"Why?"

"Because showers are girl things. We like presents and talk and admiring the gifts."

Again Julie struck a stubborn pose. "I don't like this!"

"What, dear?"

"How come you didn't tell me about these things before?"

Anna swallowed. "Um, what things?"

"These things that men can do and girls can't."

Anna sat down on the couch. "Because your daddy was seldom here and Hank was a baby so it didn't much matter. We didn't have many friends, so it was just you and me and we did the same things."

"And now we won't?"

"Yes, dear, but we'll also do other things. You like to play with Drew, don't you?"

She nodded rapidly.

"I know," Anna said with a grin. "But I can't go play with Drew."

"Why not?"

"Because he's a child and I'm an adult."

"That's stupid."

"Maybe, but we each have a category we fit in and we have to follow the rules for our group."

"I don't like this!" she said again and ran out to the porch to wait for Joe.

Anna smoothed down the sleeve of her new dress. She hoped Joe liked it. All the changes in their lives were making life difficult, but no one said it would be easy. Was she doing the right thing? She knew her answer was yes. That was obvious. Julie had learned more about life in the last couple of days than she would ever have learned if they continued as they did…alone.

But tomorrow night, she'd have to face a few changes. She hoped she didn't disappoint Joe. He said he had a low sex drive, but she had to wonder about that statement. Sometimes when he kissed her, she thought maybe he underestimated himself. What scared her most of all was that she liked it. She never liked Derek's kisses after they were married.

She was staring into space when Joe arrived. She hurried out on the porch to make sure Julie didn't say anything inappropriate. "Joe! We're ready to go. Can you help carry some of Hank's stuff—there's always so much to lug around."

"Sure, honey. Hi, peaches," he said to Julie.

"Why did you call me that?" she demanded.

"Because there is nothing prettier than a summer peach in full bloom. Just like your pretty cheeks." He smiled, but Julie didn't return that smile.

"Would you call Drew peaches?"

Joe looked surprised. "Why, no. He'd be insulted."

"Then I'm insulted, too!"

"Julie, you're being rude to Joe. Go get in Joe's truck." Then she mouthed to Joe, "I'll explain later." She was amazed at the joy those words brought. She would soon have someone to lean on. Someone to share the events of the day. A sense of loneliness she hadn't even been aware of fell away. It made her feel stronger, lighter.

A beautiful smile lit her face and she lifted her lips as Joe approached her.

Joe didn't miss the invitation and he welcomed it. He'd been worrying a lot about how Anna would react to him. She wasn't very large. He was afraid he'd scare her, but she seemed fine.

"You look beautiful, Anna."

"Thank you." She gave him an extra kiss for the compliment.

He responded, "Remind me to compliment you more often."

Julie honked the horn and Anna hurried out to give her a lecture. Joe followed with a grin on his face, carrying Hank in his carrier and other baby paraphernalia.

When they got to the Crawfords where the women were going to meet to go on to the party, Julie grabbed Drew.

Anna saw them whispering in the corner and knew the outcome wasn't going to be a happy one. She tried to hurry up the departure, but when she called Julie to come, the child whirled around, crossed her arms over her chest and announced, "No! I'm not going just because I'm a girl!"

Chapter Ten

Anna had whispered that she was having difficulty with Julie because she explained some of the new house rules. Joe still wasn't clear about what was going on, but he didn't want her upset. He scooped a stiff Julie up in his arms and walked out of the room. He pretended to almost drop Julie when they got to the porch and she grabbed him around his neck. He sat down on the porch steps and placing her on one knee, asked her what was wrong.

"I don't want to go to the shower while Drew gets to stay here and have fun. It's not fair!"

"I don't think it's fair that your mom has to go alone to that shower when she's scared."

"She's not scared," Julie protested, but she peeped over her shoulder to get a look at her mom.

"Yeah, she is. You see, she's a little nervous about

all the changes about to happen in her life. And she has to go to the party and she needs you there so she won't be alone. I'd appreciate it if you'd go with her.''

"But, Joe!"

He nodded. "I know. It's not fair. But it's not fair that Hank has to go, too. He's a boy. Boys don't go to showers!''

She began steaming again.

"Will you go with your mom and hold her hand? Please? For me?''

Julie looked over her shoulder again and then agreed. Joe drew a breath of relief. He lifted her and stood, then crossed the porch back to the waiting Anna. "Julie has changed her mind.''

"I'm so glad. Thank you, Julie, for agreeing to go.''

Julie raised her eyes to Joe and took her mom's hand in hers. "It's okay, Mommy. Don't be afraid.''

"What did you tell her?'' Anna asked, her eyes rounded in surprise.

"That you were nervous.'' He gave her a quick kiss.

Since they were sharing a car with Carol and Kelly, Anna couldn't say anything to her daughter, but the child clung so tightly to Anna's hand, she finally decided to say nothing at all. And she wondered how Joe had known.

"Now, I'll bring out the beers,'' Caleb Crawford said, "but you have to remind me to check on several things your Mama's got cooking!'' Everyone roared with laughter because Caleb was notoriously bad at remembering those kinds of details. All of his sons and son-in-law, plus Rafe, Pete's father-in-law, were there. And the husbands of other invitees to the shower were coming later. Pete and Joe went out on the back porch and stood quietly listening to the bustle inside.

"Everything okay with Julie?"

"Yeah," Joe said with a grin, leaning against a post. "Something about life not being fair. She thought she should stay here with Drew."

Pete grinned in return. "Don't look at me for advice, Joe. Alexandra's not big enough to cause problems just yet."

"Yeah. I finally caught up with you. Now I've got a four-year-old, too. It feels good, Pete!"

"I'm glad you're happy, Joe. And you knew we were jokin' about the little talk this afternoon?"

"I knew you were doing what you were told to do. I just wish I knew the reason for those orders. I'm worried about Anna. If half the things I heard about Derek are true, he was a nasty piece of work. No way Anna should've married him."

"Yeah. I imagine you'll have to go slow with her."

"Yeah."

"Should we ask Dad to explain the birds and bees to us again?"

"I don't think so," Joe said with a laugh. "He sweat so much last time I thought he was having a heart attack." They both laughed at the shared memory.

"Yeah and your talk made sense, his didn't," Pete added.

Silence fell between them. Then Joe said, "You gonna handle it any better with Drew?"

"Yeah, I am. How about you?"

"With Hank? That's a long way away. I just know Anna will have to talk with Julie. I think I'll be like those cartoons, threatening to beat up anyone who touches her."

Pete lifted his hand and Joe clapped it and gave a big yeah.

A car drove up ending their private time, and they went in with the newcomers where their dad was setting up domino and card tables where they'd spend the evening.

As was the tradition, Joe showed up at the hostesses' front door with his pickup, so he could load up the gifts and take them to the couple's future home, which in this case was Joe's house. There was a determined smile on Anna's face and a tired little girl still holding her hand.

"Joe, while we load the presents, would you hold Julie? She's very tired. But she's been very good." Anna kissed her daughter's cheek and went back into the house.

He swung her up into his arms. "Good girl. Did you have a good time?"

"It was okay," she mumbled sleepily.

"How about Hank? Did he behave himself?"

''All he did was sit there and dribble and everybody said he was so cute!'' There was an edge of disgust in her sleepiness.

''I know. It's not fair.''

''Yeah.''

''Okay. I'm going to put you in the front seat and go get Hank. It's about time I rescue him, don't you think?''

When Joe opened the door to the truck to insert the baby carrier, he found Julie curled into a ball, sound asleep. Then he grabbed the last of the gifts, saying thanks to all those he ran into. When he finally found Anna, she was telling the ladies thank-you and shaking hands. He was afraid she would faint if he didn't get her out of there soon.

Joe slid his arms around Anna and joyfully felt her lean back against him. ''I've got the kids in the truck. Are you ready to go?''

''Oh, yes,'' Anna sighed softly.

''Ladies, thank you all, but I'm taking these three to bed so they'll come to the wedding tomorrow.''

There was some applause and a few calls or warnings about jumping the gun. But his mother nodded approvingly, so he didn't worry about anyone else.

It was a silent ride, even though Anna was awake. He held her hand, loving the feel of her skin against his. ''Was it very bad?'' he finally asked.

''No. But—after a while, I thought my mouth was in a permanent smile.''

''I know the feeling,'' he said with a laugh. ''When

my grandparents used to come to visit, we had to wear our suits and sit in the living room and not get dirty. And always smile.''

Anna smiled and squeezed his hand. Then she sat up straight as he drove into her own front yard. "But I thought you were taking all the gifts to your house?''

"I am. As soon as I tuck you three in.''

"But who will help you?''

He leaned over both children and kissed her concerned lips. "I can manage the gifts, honey. Come on. Let's get the babies inside.''

He took Julie in his arms, leaving the carrier for Anna. He carried Julie up to her bed and met Anna at the bottom of the stairs. "You go dress Julie and I'll work on Hank.''

When they had both children in their jammies, they met in the hallway. Joe swooped her into his arms and carried her down the hall to her own bedroom.

"You know what? I'm glad I'm not moving in here.''

Anna leaned back to look at him. "I admit your house is nicer, but it's not a bad house.''

"That's not it.'' Joe took a deep breath and then admitted, "I don't want to use the same bed as Derek.''

At first Anna looked shocked. Then she dropped her head. "Don't worry. He didn't use it much.''

"Good.''

"Thank you for helping me put the children to bed. When Derek was going back out, he'd stop long enough for me and Julie to get out and then he'd drive off before I could even get the house unlocked. This was nice."

"What a bastard!" Joe muttered.

"Yes," she agreed calmly. "You're so much more beautiful than he was."

Joe gently kissed her lips. "I hope you always feel that way."

Her arms were around his neck and it didn't bother her at all when he carried her to her bed. But he released her as she lay on the mattress.

His voice hoarse, he said, "Anna, tomorrow I'll follow you to bed, but tonight, I'm going home and unload our gifts, okay?"

"Yes."

He leaned over and kissed her one more time. Then he promised to lock up and ran down the stairs as if he were being chased.

Anna wrapped her arms around herself and let her mind think about the future. Before she met Joe, she tried to make it through each day. The future was a scary possibility that she preferred to ignore.

She guessed Joe had given her a future for both her and her children. What a glorious man!

When the sun woke up the world on Sunday morning, Joe was already awake. He lay in his big bed, trying not to think that Anna would be lying next to him soon. Her reaction was encouraging, but he knew this marriage wasn't just about the physical. Her spirit was that of a fighter. She'd made a mistake in her first marriage, but she hadn't bailed out. She'd tried to make a go of it. And she'd fought for her children's happiness. He'd fallen for that fighting spirit. He'd fallen for the innocence he'd sensed in her. He'd fallen for her beauty, inside as well as outside. Now she would be in his care. He made a silent promise to prove himself worthy of her trust. A knock on his back door startled him.

"Coming," he called, grabbing his jeans to go open the door. He grinned when he saw Pete and Gil, his nearest neighbors, and also his brother and brother-in-law.

"What are you two doing?" he asked.

"Well, our wives are taking breakfast to Anna. We thought it only fair if you got breakfast in bed, too," Gil said.

"Thanks, but let's have it in the kitchen," Joe suggested, leading the way to his spacious kitchen. He looked at it critically.

"She'll love it, Joe. Quit worrying," Pete said, patting him on the shoulder after he'd set down what he was carrying.

"How did you know?" Joe growled.

Gil grinned. "We've both been there."

All three men exchanged a smile. Joe got down some mugs and poured the coffee they'd brought with them.

"Anna has seen it before. And she seemed to like

it. But she didn't get much time to look around. Julie hasn't even picked out her room.''

"They're going to love it,'' Pete assured him. He passed a plate of fresh crescent rolls and sausage to Joe.

"Mmm, this smells good.''

"Yeah, and you can relax. We didn't make them. You know the girls did all this. They're really excited to welcome Anna and the kids into the family.''

"Yeah,'' Gil said. ''Now we three are all married and each of us has two children.''

"Yeah,'' Pete nodded in agreement. Then he stopped, frowning, staring at Gil. ''Wait a minute! You only have one child.''

Gil beamed at the other two. ''Not anymore!''

There was a lot of hugging and back pounding while Gil told them that their sister Lindsay was pregnant again. They'd had a little boy a year after their marriage. He was now a year and a half old.

"Is it going to be a boy or a girl?'' Pete asked.

"We don't know yet. She's just two months along. The sleepy, grumpy stage.'' His smile told them he didn't mind.

Joe tried to ignore the twinge of envy he felt. He'd never had a child, never shared the birth of his child. He reprimanded himself; he was going to have a family starting today and that was more than he'd ever hoped for.

"Do you think he's told them yet?'' Kelly asked.

"Of course,'' Lindsay said. ''That's why I had to

tell Mom and Dad this morning. Gil can't keep something like that a secret. He's more excited than me."

"I think that's wonderful," Anna said. "Derek never cared, except it kept me from interfering in his life. He didn't care anything about Julie. Maybe it would've been different if he'd lived to see Hank."

"Don't fool yourself," Carol said. "Those kind don't care about anyone but themselves."

"You're right," Anna said softly, hanging her head.

"But I can guarantee Joe would be over the moon if he thought—" Carol broke off and said, "more coffee, dear?"

"Yes, please. I feel so lazy. This is lovely." Kelly, Lindsay and Carol had awakened her this morning with breakfast. She'd chosen to have it in the kitchen. The children had gone with Caleb, much to Anna's surprise. "I'm surprised Mr. Crawford was willing to take the children."

"He's always willing to help out. He's very happy for Joe."

Anna smiled, but it wobbled a little. "I hope I can make him happy."

Carol patted her hand. "You do make him happy, Anna. You make all of us happy. Now, time for your bubble bath. Then we're going to give you a manicure and pedicure before it's time to dress."

"Oh! That's lovely. But my nails aren't long," she said, staring at her nails doubtfully.

"Don't worry," Lindsay said. "It will be your

choice whether we put color on them or not, but it makes me feel good to have mine done.''

"I've never had a pedicure.''

"They are the best. Carol paid for me to go to the shop. It made me feel wonderful,'' Kelly said with a smile.

Carol said, "I would have sent you to the shop, but there was such short notice I couldn't get you an appointment. You'll have to make do with our best efforts.''

"I'm sure it will be wonderful,'' Anna replied.

Anna spent a wonderful morning with the ladies. Unfortunately, it didn't calm her fears about making Joe happy.

The late spring sun shone through the stained glass windows of the old church as Joe Crawford stood with the pastor and waited for Anna Pointer to join them at the altar. Anna stared at the big man she was to marry, a man who thought he wasn't handsome enough for her. He looked wonderful; he was a good man and she silently promised him her best efforts to make him happy. She was sure he would do the same for her.

She and Julie walked down the aisle together. Julie, too, watched Joe. Her child had recognized his goodness before Anna had. She'd been fighting everyone too much at first. Julie had known almost at once what a good father Joe would be.

Julie shifted her gaze to Anna and squeezed her

hand. Anna smiled at her daughter and Julie whispered, "Hank doesn't get to come with us."

"He'll join us down there. Lindsay is holding him."

Julie worrying about her brother gave Anna a warm feeling. She wanted Julie to have the family relationships that the Crawfords had. Her two sisters-in-law were wonderful. And she'd met the third earlier, Abby. She lived in Texas near Wichita Falls, only a couple of hours away. She seemed as nice as Kelly and Lindsay.

Julie was going to have lots of cousins. She would never be alone again. None of them would. When they'd reached the altar, Anna looked up at Joe and smiled at him. He reached for her hand.

After the pastor read the traditional vows, Joe bent down and kissed Anna. That hungry kiss, not the sweet ones. When he lowered her, he picked up Julie and kissed her cheek. Then Lindsay stepped forward with Hank. Joe took the little boy in his arms and gently kissed his forehead. Then he took Anna's hand, she took Julie's, and all four of them walked down the aisle to a surprisingly full church.

Joe squared his shoulders. He was a family man now, and he liked the way it felt. He was a married man, too, and he liked that even better. They were having a simple reception at the church with cake and punch. Then he and Anna would go to his house. He was ready to begin his new life.

They stood in line together, without the children, who tired quickly. Joe introduced her to people she'd never met even though she'd lived there almost five years. He had his arm around her and he acted as if she were a princess. Anna leaned against him, drawing strength from him.

"Are you too tired?" he whispered in her ear.

"No, if you don't mind me leaning against you."

"I love it," he whispered and kissed her. Several people cheered and Anna's cheeks bloomed.

When they moved to cut the wedding cake a few minutes later, Joe took the frosting on his finger and delicately put it in Anna's mouth so she could savor the sweetness.

She returned the favor, neither interested in making a mess on each other with the icing. Suddenly Anna was sure her marriage to Joe would be as sweet as the icing. It was a wonderful thought.

Carol cut them each a piece of cake and shooed them over to chairs to sit and eat it.

After a couple of minutes, Anna said, "Why is no one talking to us?"

Joe chuckled. "They think we want to be alone."

"Oh."

"Don't worry. You don't have to do anything. We'll leave after we finish our cake."

"Okay. Where are the children?"

"Julie and Drew are eating cake under Mom's supervision and Hank is giving Gil some practice. They're fine. Mom's taking both of them home with her."

"I know."

"So we can be alone."

She nodded.

"Anna, you're not scared of me, are you?"

"No, Joe. I'm looking forward to being alone with you."

He stared at her, as if surprised by her answer. Then his gaze intensified and he pulled her to her feet. "I think you've had enough cake. Time for us to go home," he said.

Chapter Eleven

"Do you want to wait?" Joe asked softly, hovering over Anna at the door to his bedroom.

Confused, afraid she'd misread his desire, she swallowed and said, "If you want to."

Joe picked her up, bringing her face even with his. "What I want, Anna, always, is for you to be honest with me. That's all."

"Then I don't want to wait. And I thought you didn't, either."

Relief flooded his face. "You are exactly right!" He hurried to the king-size bed, standing her on the bed.

"Joe! I'll get the bed dirty!"

"No, you won't, Anna. You're an angel and angels don't get anything dirty. You look so pretty in your pink dress!"

"Thank you, Joe. Your suit is very nice, too."

He grimaced as he ran his hands down the sides of her body. "Even I can't destroy the look of a plain suit."

"Joe Crawford! You looked so handsome in the church I couldn't stand it! Don't you dare say anything like that to me ever again," she insisted, taking his face into her hands. "You have the heart of a good man, and that's more important than any handsome face."

"As long as you're satisfied, Angel, I'll be satisfied," he whispered before he took her lips with his.

They made glorious love, neither needing instruction. Yet the depth of their enjoyment made it feel like a first for both of them. Anna loved it…for the first time. Joe loved it, too, more because this was his woman, his wife, a feeling he'd never had before. When he turned to her a second time only a few minutes later, she pushed back from him. "Joe, you lied to me about a low sex drive, didn't you?"

"Not exactly," he hedged. "I kept my sex drive under control."

She gently kissed his lips. "I'm glad."

"Are you sure you don't mind a second time?" he whispered. "I can—"

"No, I don't mind. I insist," she said with a soft, sexy chuckle. His eyes lit with joy and he gave in to her demands.

They dozed a little. Joe awoke, lying there a few minutes, contemplating his life. Then he slid out of bed as Anna awoke. "What's wrong?" she asked. "Where are you going?"

"Mom said she'd leave a picnic basket full of food on the breakfast table. I thought we'd have supper in bed. Would you like that?"

"Oh, yes, but I'm being spoilt. I could've fixed dinner."

Joe grinned slowly. His wife. He kissed her cheek. "I think you could use a little spoiling. The last couple of years must've been hard."

"It was worth it with you as my reward," she whispered. That response deserved another of those hungry kisses and it was a while before he got downstairs to find the picnic basket as promised.

Anna felt sure she was living in Paradise. The children were very happy, living in Joe's nice house, having a mother who wasn't constantly worried about their survival, having people who came in and out of the house like family, as they were. They also went places together. They went to church every Sunday and grocery shopping as a family. Joe loved accompanying them. They left Hank with Carol and Caleb, and went to see a children's movie one Friday night, accompanied by Drew. Julie loved that.

"Joe? Tonight was so much fun!" Julie exclaimed as Joe tucked her in and gave her a good-night kiss.

"Yeah, it was. I'm glad you enjoyed it. You're okay with everything since we got married?"

"There's just one thing."

Joe's heart missed a beat. "What, honey? What's wrong?"

"I don't get to call you Daddy. Mommy told Hank to call you Daddy. Drew calls Pete Daddy."

Relief ran through him. "I'd love for you to call me Daddy if you want to. I didn't want you to think we'd forgotten your real daddy."

"I don't remember him much. He wasn't very nice. You're lots better!"

"Well, thank you very much!" he exclaimed, giving her another kiss. "Now, get to sleep before we both get in trouble with your mother."

He started down the stairs, thinking about Julie's request. He needed to discuss it with Anna. Would it bother her? He'd tried to make everything perfect since their marriage. He would die if she ever left him.

He got to the bottom of the stairs. They'd formed the habit of having a cup of decaf coffee each evening before they went to bed, giving them time to discuss the day. Except for their time in bed, it was his favorite time of the day.

"Anna?" he called as he came down the hallway.

"In here," she called softly from the kitchen.

In the kitchen, he found two mugs of coffee on the table along with two pieces of cake. "Who made cake?"

"Your mother, of course. She's afraid I'm starving you to death."

Joe chuckled and put his arms around her. "She

knows better than that. Probably afraid I'm not spoiling you enough.''

She'd been rinsing dishes. She wiped her hands dry and turned around in his arms. "No, you spoil me…and I like it.''

"Good. Uh, Julie had a complaint tonight.''

"A complaint after going to the movies for the first time in her life? How could she? You bought her candy and popcorn and Coke.''

He led her to the table and sat down with her. "It didn't have to do with going to the movie. She—she wanted to call me daddy.''

Anna stared at him. "And that's a problem?''

"Not for me. I like the idea.''

Anna sighed in relief. "I like the idea, if you do.''

"I do,'' he said solemnly.

She gave him a soft smile and leaned over the table to kiss him. "Did you tell her it's okay?''

"Yes, I did.''

"That's settled then.''

"Is it? What about adopting her and Hank?''

Anna nibbled on her bottom lip. "You don't have to do that.''

He leaned back in his chair. "No, I don't, but I want to. I don't ever want either of them to have any doubt that I married all three of you. For life.''

Anna blinked faster, trying to hold back tears. "You are such a good man, Joe.''

"No, I'm being selfish. I want Julie and Hank to belong to both of us, not just you.''

"I'm willing, but shouldn't we wait until we've been married a while?" she asked, doubt still in her eyes.

"No. I don't need to test them to see if they're good enough."

"I didn't mean—okay. That will be fine. And shouldn't we talk about protection? I haven't been on the Pill in several years. Do you want me to see the doctor?"

Joe knew what he wanted to say, but he was sure he should be careful. "Is it too soon after Hank? He's almost a year old."

"No, it's not too soon. If…if you want more children."

"Yeah, I'd like about half a dozen," he said, watching her reaction carefully.

"Oh! Well, I—I guess that would be good."

"As long as they don't look like me?" he asked because he was unhappy with her response.

She glared at him. "I told you not to talk like that!"

"Honey, you don't have to pretend. I know I'm not—"

Before he could finish that sentence, Anna threw her arms around his neck and gave him a demanding, sexy kiss. When she lifted her head, she said, "I'm ready for bed."

"But you haven't finished your cake," he said, his gaze on her lips.

"Come on," she whispered, pulling him from his chair toward the stairs.

He didn't argue anymore.

The warm summer changed to cooler weather as September marched into their lives. Julie and Drew began preschool, readying themselves for that magical step into kindergarten. Hank was walking, getting into everything and, of course, calling Joe daddy.

Anna was unhappy.

Joe had married her for a family. He wanted six children. After three months of marriage, Anna hadn't gotten pregnant. She'd also delayed his adopting her children. Because she knew she'd have to leave him if she couldn't give him what he wanted. She loved him too much to deny him anything. She loved him so much more than she had when she'd married him.

Joe accepted her postponing the adoption without any questions, which told her he knew why. Every month she waited, crossing her fingers that she would be pregnant. Finally, this month, her period didn't come and she was waiting to test for her pregnancy. She was so tense, she scarcely responded to Joe. After picking Julie up from preschool, they stopped by Joe's parents' house and found Caleb and Carol in the kitchen with a stranger. Anna shook his hand, but she didn't know him and assumed he was a local she hadn't met yet. She was friendly so as not to arouse suspicions. He moved too close to her and rattled off compliments that were ridiculous. She used Julie as an excuse and left the room. When she returned a few minutes later, Joe seemed upset. She suggested they go home and he agreed.

In the car, she demanded to know what was wrong.

"So you hope he gets the job?"

She tried to shuffle through the words he'd spoken, but nothing made sense. "What job?"

"Dad's thinking of hiring a manager for the ranch so he doesn't have to work so hard. And you wished him luck."

"I was trying to be nice," she said, still confused.

"I should've known."

"Should've known what?"

"Are you fighting?" Julie asked, the glow removed from her face, replaced by alarm.

That got Anna's attention. All along she told herself she had married Joe for her children's sake, trying to hide even from herself the love she felt for the strong man beside her. "No! Of course not, Julie. Daddy is upset by something I said, but I don't even know what."

"Oh, really?" Joe cut back, his sarcasm unabated. "You don't think I should object to a man ogling my wife...or my wife ogling him."

"Ogling him?" Anna repeated.

"What's ogging him?" Julie asked.

"Never mind, honey. Daddy and I will talk about it later. It's nothing for you to worry about." Anna crossed her arms over her chest, hoping she'd made her point and Joe would drop whatever was upsetting him until they could talk alone.

And maybe, just maybe, she could prove to Joe he hadn't made a mistake marrying her. She'd worked so hard to please him. She kept his beautiful house spotless. She'd made sure her children behaved properly. And she'd tried so hard to get pregnant.

It was only fair that he get what he wanted because he'd been so good to her and her children. She hoped she'd be pregnant when she took the home test in the morning. She said a short prayer that she would be.

Joe understood what Anna wanted. She wanted to keep their life perfect. It had taken him a while to realize something was wrong. After all, everything was perfect. How could he complain?

But he noticed that she wouldn't even let one glass sit in the kitchen sink dirty. She made the bed as soon as she got up. She never stayed in bed a minute late. His clothes barely had time to go through the laundry before they were hanging in his closet, fresh and ready to go. He'd try to get her to relax, but she wouldn't. He was beginning to wonder what was wrong with her.

When he talked to his mother, she suggested he relax. He tried to explain that his relaxing wasn't the problem. He made love to Anna almost every night. But he was very careful not to say he loved her, even though he did desperately. He didn't want to put any pressure on her. She had married him to give her children a good home.

He'd thought that would be a fair exchange, he'd have a beautiful wife and the family he'd dreamed of.

And he'd provide for them. It seemed a simple plan. It seemed like it was working…wasn't it?

No, it wasn't. He didn't understand why, but he wasn't making Anna happy. She seemed to grow more tense as time passed. If he didn't do something soon, he was afraid he'd lose her.

Anna was wiping down the cabinets that evening after having put the children to bed. Joe had promised to read them a story, something he did frequently. Julie loved it. Hank tried to read with Joe, pointing to the pictures and babbling. Anna smiled, thinking about her son and Joe. He was so gentle with him. Yet he encouraged him to be tough and grow strong.

He did the opposite with Julie, encouraging her femininity.

He was a wonderful father.

"What are you thinking of?" a rough voice demanded.

Anna almost dropped the dish she was putting away. "Oh! You scared me to death. I almost dropped this glass." She smiled at Joe.

He didn't return her smile. "Tell me!" he demanded.

She didn't understand his harsh tones. But she explained. Why not? "I was thinking about what a good daddy you are."

"You weren't either!" he snapped. "You were thinking about *him!*"

Anna stared at him, trying to figure out what he was

referring to. "You mean Hank? Well, yes, I guess so. After all—"

"No!" Joe responded in a full roar. He'd never spoken like that before.

Anna took a step backward.

"Don't move away. I saw how you looked at him."

She straightened her shoulders and stepped closer to him again. "Who are you talking about?"

"That man you wanted my father to hire as manager, that's who. That Hollywood-handsome man in my mother's kitchen!"

Anna blinked several times, trying to comprehend what Joe was saying. "You—you're talking about that man at your father's today? What about him? Why would I be thinking about him?"

"Don't give me that innocent look!" Joe exclaimed, exactly because that was the look that tugged at his heart. "You were flirting with him!"

She still looked lost, as if his words were incomprehensible. "Joe, my mind was on something else completely. I was just trying to be polite."

"Polite, huh! What were you thinking about?"

"I—I can't tell you." She was going to take the test in the morning. She wouldn't want to raise false hopes. Or to remind him of her failure to give him children.

"You mean, you won't tell me." Joe snapped. "You want him instead of me!"

She drew a deep breath, trying to keep the situation

under control. "Joe, have I ever made you feel that I didn't like your lovemaking?"

"No! But obviously you're a good actress!"

"Joe!" Anna exclaimed, cut to the heart by his words. "Joe, I—I'm not pretending."

Joe ignored her and stormed out of the kitchen.

Anna stood there, leaning against the cabinet, trembling, trying to figure out what had just happened. Then she leaned over, clutching her stomach as sharp pain shot through her.

She instinctively started to call Joe. Then she remembered his abrupt departure. She had to call the doctor.

Because she thought she was having a miscarriage.

Joe tossed and turned most of the night. At one point, he heard a vehicle, but he checked to see if Julie and Hank were still in their beds. He at least knew Anna that well. She wouldn't leave for good without her babies.

But she might go meet another man.

When the phone rang an hour later, it was his father.

"Dad, what's wrong?"

"You mean besides Anna?"

"What do you mean besides Anna? Where is she?"

"She should be in the hospital by now. I'm waiting for them to call. Why didn't you go with her? I would've come over to stay with the kids."

Joe drew a deep breath. "What are you talking about, Dad?"

"Your wife arrives here bleeding to death and you don't know what's wrong?" his father said in exasperation.

"Get over here, Dad, and keep an eye on the kids for me."

With the phone tucked behind his ear, Joe was pulling on a pair of jeans. "I'll wait for you at the back door."

He slammed down the phone receiver without waiting for an answer. Anna almost bled to death? Why? She wasn't hurt when he went to bed. True, he'd upset her. She'd upset him, too. But blood? He was still buttoning his shirt as his father's truck came up the drive. He rushed out and crawled into his own truck.

The drive to the small hospital in Lawton had never taken so long, but he drove as quickly as possible. He pulled into the emergency area and parked his truck haphazardly. He was almost in the building before his truck door shut.

"My wife! Anna Crawford!" he demanded.

"Your wife is with the doctor. I'm sure he'll come out and see you when he can. Just have a seat."

"He doesn't even know I'm here. And it's her I want to see!"

"You can discuss that with the doctor. I'll let him know you're here. Please take a seat, Mr. Crawford."

Joe didn't know what else to do. He backed to the row of plastic chairs and sat down. He watched as the nurse left her desk for only a couple of minutes. When she came back she waved to him.

He leaped from his chair.

"Doctor says your wife has stabilized and he thinks she's out of danger."

Relief filled him but he knew he wouldn't believe those words until he saw Anna himself.

He returned to those miserable plastic chairs and tried to be patient.

Chapter Twelve

Dr. Patrick Wilson came into view as he approached the reception desk. Joe didn't wait to see if he'd call for him. He jumped up and reached the desk in two seconds. "Pat!"

"Joe, I'm glad you're here."

"Can I see Anna?"

"Of course you can…as soon as I talk to you."

"Please tell me what's wrong?" Joe asked, worriedly. Anna was the most important person in his life.

"Well, the miscarriage—" Pat began.

"What?" Joe grabbed Patrick's scrubs and practically lifted him off the floor.

"Didn't you know? I wondered why you let her come in by herself. She almost bled to death."

"When I went upstairs, she was fine. I don't understand." He felt a sinking sensation in his stomach. "What happened?"

It seemed the floor was coming up to meet him, but the tight hold of Pat's hands saved him.

"Get a chair," he ordered someone, and suddenly Joe was sitting in one of the plastic chairs and Pat was shoving his head down between his knees. "Don't lift your head until the room stops spinning."

Slowly Joe lifted his head, trying to put what information he had into context. "I didn't even know she was pregnant. She was fine when I left her. We—we had a small argument, but—"

"Ah," the doctor nodded.

"I made her miscarry the baby?" Joe asked, tears in his eyes.

"I can't say that. Sometimes stress can be a contributing factor. But most miscarriages are nature's way of dealing with a problematic pregnancy. Hadn't you discussed a possible pregnancy?"

"Apparently not," Carol Crawford said coolly from behind Patrick.

"Mom! Were you with Anna? Is she all right? Did you leave her alone?" Joe demanded.

"Yes, I did. She has a nurse with her and she's gone to sleep. There wasn't anything I could do for her and I thought you might need me, even if you don't deserve my concern."

"But I didn't know! She never told me! I—I got jealous because she was so friendly with that handsome guy Dad was interviewing."

"Oh, Joe, for a smart man, you are so dumb!"

He shoved his hands through his hair. "Mom, you

don't understand. She's grown unhappy and I don't know what to do. I can't make her happy.''

Carol frowned, hearing the misery in her son's voice. ''Something's wrong here. You two aren't communicating.''

''She doesn't want to communicate,'' Joe said with his head down. He knew it was his fault, everything. He had tried to make her happy, but it hadn't worked. He loved her and the kids so much. He'd wanted to adopt them, but she'd put it off. That's the first time he realized she might leave him.

''Please, I need to see her? I can't upset her, or make her unhappy if she's asleep. Mom can come with me. Just let me see her,'' he pleaded to Patrick.

''Of course, you can see her. They're taking her up to a room in about ten minutes. Go in there, and go with her to the room.''

''Wait! You said she's okay!'' Joe said, his voice intense. ''Why does she need a room?''

''Joe, when you almost bleed to death, there's a recovery period. She'll probably just stay a couple of days. We'll take care of her, monitor her condition and send her home when she can recover quickly.''

Joe muttered ''Thanks'' as he turned and hurried to Anna's side. When he saw her for the first time, he came to an abrupt halt. She was so pale! The reality of Patrick's words struck him again. After staring at her for a minute, he walked slowly to her side and cautiously took her hand in his, bringing it to his lips. ''Anna, I'm sorry,'' he whispered.

"What are you apologizing for?" Carol asked, having followed him.

"I don't know. I just know she's very unhappy. I wanted to take care of her, to make life good for her. Instead, I've ruined it."

"I don't understand. You love each other, don't you?"

"I love her, Mom, but she just wanted a good life for her children. But she won't let me adopt them. That's when I realized she wasn't happy. And she's gotten very tense. I've asked her what's wrong, but she won't tell me anything."

Carol reached over to push Anna's blond hair back from her beautiful face. "I don't know about now, but when you married, she said she loved you."

Joe's heart leaped and then settled back down to it's normal beat. "Of course, she told you that. You're my mother."

"Joe, I believed her. And I thought you loved her."

"I did! I do. But I want her to be happy."

The curtains parted and a nurse entered to escort Anna to her room. "Good evening," she said with a smile.

Joe nodded. "Dr. Wilson said I could accompany my wife to her room."

"Of course. Just follow us."

Joe and Carol walked behind the bed, with its silent occupant and the nurse and orderly.

"Are you going to stay with Anna?" Carol asked.

"I want to," Joe replied.

"Fine. Once she's settled, I'll go back home and

pack a bag for her. And one for you, too. Then I'll let everyone know. Is it okay if Julie and Hank stay with us until Anna goes home?"

"Do you mind? Give them a hug from me and tell them—" he paused to gain control of his wavering voice. "Tell them I'm taking care of Mommy."

"Yes, dear." Carol patted his arm, a worried look on her face.

Joe stayed by Anna's bed until the sun rose and his mother brought their things. With the nurse's help, he dressed Anna in a soft cotton gown while she was still too groggy to do it herself. He finger-brushed her hair out of her eyes then he let her continue to sleep.

About eight, they brought her breakfast. To Joe's surprise, they even brought a tray for him.

The nurse grinned at his expression. "I snuck this out of the cafeteria. You need to keep your strength up so you can take care of her. It makes sense."

He thanked her, but turned away from his tray to feed Anna, hoping she would let him. "Anna? You need to wake up and eat now." He waited until her eyes fluttered open. Then he raised the bed and cheerfully continued with mundane details.

"Wh-where am I?"

"You're at the hospital, sweetheart. Mom brought you and Dad came to get me."

"S-sorry."

"Nothing to be concerned about…except getting well. Here, eat your eggs."

They didn't talk anymore. Joe couldn't think of anything to say. Anna didn't seem to have the energy.

She ate about half her breakfast, then she said she couldn't eat any more. "Will you at least drink your milk? You need to get more color in you before Julie and Hank come to see you."

"Will they?"

"I'd bet Julie's trying to bribe mom already. And you know how she can wrap Dad around her little finger. I bet they'll come after their naps today."

"And then I can go home?" she asked with such yearning that Joe wanted to say yes.

"Uh, I think the doctor said a couple of days."

"Oh. I'm sorry to be so much trouble."

Joe took her hand. "You're not any trouble. I just didn't know anything was wrong," he lied. He'd known something was wrong, but not this. "We want to get you well again."

"Did—did I do any damage?"

"What do you mean?" Joe asked, not sure what she was asking.

"To my body."

"Doc didn't say so. You'll have to ask him."

"When—when will he be here?"

"I don't know, Anna. He'll probably be by later."

He watched as her eyelids settled over her blue eyes. "Are you going back to sleep?"

She gave a slight nod. Then she didn't move.

Joe watched the rise and fall of her chest to indicate she had fallen asleep. Then he ate his breakfast. Stacking the two trays together, he returned to her side.

The next time Anna awoke, she saw darkness out her hospital window. And Lindsay was the one beside her.

"Lindsay? What are you doing here?"

"Waiting for you to wake up. How are you?"

Anna smiled weakly. It wasn't a big one, but at least it was still there. "I think I'm doing better. Where's Joe?"

"He stayed until about two. I insisted he go home and take a nap so he could see the kids and reassure them."

"Oh. That's good. Are they okay?"

"I think so. They're at mom's. Do you want to call them?" Lindsay offered, smiling.

"I can do that?"

"Of course," Lindsay said with a smile. She eased herself out of the chair to bring the phone over.

"You should be home resting, Lindsay. You have to take care of your baby," Anna said. "Please, I don't want you to—" she broke off and was interrupted by Lindsay's reassurance.

"Anna, I'm fine. All I've done is sit in this chair. I even took a little nap myself." She dialed her parents' number.

"Mom? Anna wants to talk to her children. Are they up from their naps?"

Anna waited anxiously. She'd never been away from her children, except when she had Hank. Julie had stayed with her grandparents for two days and been miserable. When Julie's voice came on the phone, she almost wept with relief.

"Mommy, how are you? Grammy said you were sick."

"Just a little bit, Julie. Are you and Hank doing all right?"

"Sure. Grammy and Grandpa are taking good care of us. Daddy picked me up from school and then he went home to take a nap." Julie giggled. "I didn't know daddies took naps."

"I'm afraid he didn't get much sleep last night. Promise me you'll be good for Grammy, okay? And help with Hank. I'll be home in a few days."

"I will, Mommy."

"I love you, Julie. Kiss Hank for me."

"I love you, Mommy."

Anna handed the phone back to Lindsay and closed her eyes. Such a simple thing and she was exhausted. She wanted to talk to Joe. But she wouldn't call him. He was probably fed up with her. That argument about some man, she couldn't even remember who, was so weird. She thought he was trying to get rid of her. She couldn't ask him that.

She suddenly realized Lindsay was talking to her mother. She frowned. "Is anything wrong?" she whispered, but Lindsay shook her head.

When Lindsay hung up the phone, she said, "Joe is going to bring Julie to see you this evening after dinner."

Anna felt panic rush through her, which was ridiculous. She wanted to see Joe. But she was afraid he'd tell her he didn't want to be married anymore. "O-okay."

"Is something wrong? Is it too soon for visitors?"

Lindsay asked and Anna knew she hadn't done a good job hiding her worry.

"No, it's not too soon. I'd love the visit. But the call made me very tired, so I guess I'd better take another nap." She smiled at Lindsay. "You'd better go home and take a real nap, too."

"Well, I think I will, if you don't mind."

"Of course not. I'll just be sleeping."

Once Lindsay had left, Anna wearily closed her eyes, trying to think about the future. It all depended on Joe. If he didn't want her anymore, she'd have to pack up and leave, but thinking about that was so hard. Her body couldn't hold in the tension as sleep took over.

Joe hesitated in the hospital hallway. "Julie, you know your mommy is sick, so she may look a little pale. But don't worry. She's going to be all right."

"Okay. Grammy told me."

"Oh. And—if anything is wrong, tell me, not Mommy, okay?"

"Okay."

He opened the door to Anna's room. She was sitting halfway up with her dinner tray before her, but he couldn't tell if she'd eaten anything. "Evening, Anna. We thought you'd be through with your dinner."

"I am. Julie! I'm so glad to see you!"

Joe held Julie up so Anna could hug her. Then he set Julie on the side of the bed and picked up the fork from the tray. "You know, you have to eat to build your strength, so we'll talk while you eat. Julie, tell Mommy what you did at school today.''

Julie loved to talk about her adventures and she launched into the story she'd already told Joe while he placed small bites of the meat loaf in Anna's mouth. He alternated the meat loaf with a salad and beans.

After about fifteen minutes of Julie telling about her day, he suggested she tell her mother about Hank. He switched to feeding Anna some apple pie.

Anna interrupted Julie. ''Joe, I don't need the pie. I'm full.''

''You have to build your strength. What did you have for lunch?''

She looked surprised and then worried. ''I don't remember.''

''I should've stayed to make sure you ate,'' he muttered to himself.

''No. No, I was sleeping. That's all I do. Except I remember Lindsay was here.''

''Yeah. The family is going to space out their visits so you won't get too tired.''

''That's very nice of them, but I hate to be so much trouble.''

Joe drew a deep breath. ''Anna, you're family, remember? They all wanted to come at once, but I suggested they space it out. We let Lindsay come first because we didn't want her worrying about you. Not while she's—I mean…''

''I know what you mean. Joe—I can explain—''

''Not now,'' he replied, nodding at Julie who was

watching them intently. "Besides, you didn't do anything wrong. We just want you to get well. Right, Julie?"

She nodded enthusiastically. "Grandpa has a baby horse. He's beautiful. Grandpa said maybe I should have my own horse, like for a birthday present. He said he'd ask daddy. Did he, Daddy?"

Joe shrugged his shoulders at Anna in apology. "He did, Julie, but I told him we'd have to talk with Mommy. And now's not the time to worry Mommy."

"Why would it worry her?" Julie wanted to know.

"Because you're too little," Anna hurriedly said, disturbed by this subject.

"But I'll be *five!*" Julie said, making five sound ancient.

Joe laughed and Anna mustered a small smile. "No discussing it tonight, young lady," Joe said. "Your mommy is too tired."

Before Julie could say anything, he swung her to the floor. "Tell Mommy good-night."

She asked to be held up so she could kiss her mother. Joe did so, then lowered her to the floor again. He dropped a kiss on Anna's forehead and told her he would see her in the morning. Then he and Julie left the room.

Once they were in the truck, he said, "I think I'll have a talk with Grandpa. He mustn't discuss things like horses with you instead of me first. And I don't want you discussing that with your mommy until she's well. Okay?"

"But I don't understand why she would be upset. Drew has a horse."

"No more. Mommy and I make the decisions concerning you. Pete and Kelly make decisions for Drew."

"Is it because I'm a girl?" she demanded, her hands on her hips. Joe thought she looked exactly like her mommy at that moment, her chin lifted in the air.

"Nope. It means we need time to make our decisions and Mommy doesn't feel like thinking about these things right now." He pulled into his parents' front yard. "Come on, Grammy will be fussing at us if we don't get you in bed on time."

Julie giggled. "I know. She says if I don't sleep a lot, I won't grow."

"She told me the same thing," Joe said with a smile.

"Oooh, that's scary. I don't want to grow as big as you, Daddy!" Then she burst into giggles that lasted all the way into the house.

"Well, I guess the visit was good for her," Carol said, her brows raised slightly.

"It was good for both of us. I fed Anna some supper. She hadn't eaten much of anything. I'll stop in again after I take Julie to school and feed her her breakfast."

"Good. Kelly is going in before the store opens to visit, too. Maybe she can stay for lunch."

With both his parents watching him anxiously, all he could do was agree and kiss Julie good-night. Then he stopped by Hank's room. The boy had already gone to sleep and Joe missed spending time with him. These two children had become so important to his life. He couldn't think about life without them. Life without Anna was worse than anything. What was he going to do?

She was going home today! Anna still tired easily, but after three days of bed rest, constantly being fed, she needed to get up and around. The doctor had given her instructions. Stay in bed most of the time and try to get up just a little bit each day. He'd said there was no reason she couldn't have another child. But not yet. She was not to be intimate with Joe for at least a month.

He was coming to get her. She anxiously watched the door. When she heard heavy footsteps in the hall, she knew he was there. "Joe?" she called eagerly.

He walked in, a grin on his face. "You ready to come home?"

"Oh, yes, please."

"Need help with anything?"

"No, the nurse helped me dress. It's ridiculous that I need help, but I'll get better quickly at home."

"If you follow doctor's orders," he said in a warning tone.

"Of course, I will."

"I know. I have the cleaning lady coming every day so you won't feel the need to tidy anything. Besides, we can survive a dirty glass in the sink or baby's toys on the floor."

"I thought one of the reasons you married me was to keep house for you," she said slowly.

He was about to reassure her when Patrick came in, followed by a nurse with a wheelchair. "Good morning. I know, I know," the doctor said, "you're happy to be going home. It hurts my feelings."

Anna's cheeks turned pink. "Sorry, Dr. Wilson. But I'm glad to go home. I need to see my children."

He laughed. "That's the way it should be. But you remember my rules. I want to see you in a week looking even more healthy than you are now. Take things easy, okay?"

"Yes, of course."

Joe shook his hand and thanked him again, and Patrick slapped him on the shoulder. "No problem. Goodbye."

She was seated in the wheelchair, in spite of telling them she could walk that far. Even Joe agreed with them. She settled in the chair and sat back while the nurse pushed her out of the hospital.

Joe followed along, carrying her suitcase and the vases of flowers the family had sent. When they reached the truck, Joe lifted her out of the wheelchair and set her on the truck seat.

"I could've gotten up here by myself, Joe," she said.

"No need."

It seemed as time passed, that he had grown less talkative. He'd visited several times each day, but he either brought Julie with him, or someone else was visiting at the same time.

In the truck, alone for the first time, she didn't say anything either. Leaning back against the seat, she took deep breaths, trying to conserve her energy for the arrival home.

"Is Julie going to be there?" she finally asked.

"She'll be there soon. Dad was going to pick her up."

"They've done so much for me."

"For us."

"Yes, of course."

When they reached the house, the housekeeper opened the door as Joe carried her into the house. "Mornin' Miz Crawford," she said with a big smile. "Welcome home."

"Thank you, Edith."

"Your bed's ready for you."

"Thank you," she said again, unsure what else to say.

"Please fix her a cup of tea with a small plate of those cookies mom made yesterday and bring it up to her," Joe directed.

She started to protest such cosseting, but then she realized she was a little hungry. "I think I'm going to gain too much weight if I'm not careful."

"I don't think so. But we would like you to look a little less starved. People will say I'm not taking care of you," he said with a grin.

Upstairs, he put her down on the bed, its covers turned back and the pillows piled up for her to lean on.

"I need to scoot over a little, Joe. I'm in the center of the bed. I haven't left room for you."

"Not a problem. I've moved my things to the spare room down the hall."

Anna grew still. "You have?"

"I thought that way I wouldn't wake you up in the mornings," Joe said.

But Anna knew differently. He didn't want her anymore. The joy of coming home was lost because now she knew this definitely wasn't her home. As soon as she got strong, she'd be leaving, along with her children.

Anna had been home five days. Joe wasn't sure what he'd done wrong, but she scarcely spoke to him when he visited her room. She asked Edith for anything she needed.

He felt she was slipping away from him and he didn't know what to do. This morning he'd gone out to work before she awoke as usual, but he'd decided to join her while she had breakfast.

"Morning, Edith. Do you have Anna's breakfast tray ready to go up to her?"

"No, Joe. She insisted on coming down to eat, and she's already finished."

. Joe stared at the woman. "But she's supposed to— the doctor said—never mind. I'll go talk to her."

He took the stairs two at a time and burst into the master bedroom before Anna had realized anyone was there.

He came to an abrupt halt when he discovered Anna

filling a suitcase. "Going somewhere?" he asked, his voice hard.

She jumped and almost fell over as she turned around. "Joe! I didn't think you'd be in until lunch."

"Obviously. What are you doing, Anna? You're too weak to even think of traveling. And where would you go? Julie can't miss school, and you can't carry Hank. He's too big."

Anger was building up in him. He couldn't believe she'd walk out like that!

"I have to go, Joe."

"Why?"

"Because I can't give you what you want. We both know that." She turned away, as if she had tears in her eyes. But she was the one breaking his heart, not the other way around.

"What are you talking about?"

She began packing again and he tore across the room and ripped the clothes from her hand. "Stop it! Stop trying to leave me. Anna, I'll try harder. Just tell me what you want. You have to communicate with me. I can't guess what's wrong, but I don't want you to leave."

"Joe, I'm not stupid. You moved into another bedroom. Action speaks louder than words."

He stared at her. "I did that because the doctor said we shouldn't—I was afraid I'd upset you. I wanted you to rest and get well."

"I could have done that a lot better if you'd held me every night," she said softly, her gaze on the suitcase.

Joe leaned closer, not sure he heard right. "Then why didn't you tell me?"

"Because you left me here all alone. I'm not dumb, Joe."

As if afraid he was making a wrong conclusion, he slowly put his arms around her. "Anna, I've wanted to hold you close every night, but I didn't think I should."

She leaned against his big chest, her eyes closed. Finally, she whispered, "I've missed you so."

His arms tightened. "Dear God, Anna, I've missed you. I can't get to sleep because you're not there. And I've been so scared that you were going to leave me. That's why I began an argument about that stupid man my dad interviewed. I wanted you to tell me you—" He broke off.

She raised her head. "What did you want me to tell you?"

"That you love me like I love you."

"You love me?" she asked, her voice disbelieving.

"Of course, I love you. I've loved you almost since the beginning. I've never felt like this about anyone. It took me by surprise and I was afraid to tell you. When you agreed to marry me for your children's sake, I figured I'd gotten lucky and—"

"Joe Crawford! You dufus! I love you! I've loved you since before we got married! You thought I'd marry you so you'd take care of my kids? I can't believe—"

Joe's lips covered her in one of those hungry kisses

she loved. Her arms went around his neck and she clung to him.

When he finally released her, he said, "We've got to stop this because the doctor said not for a month."

"You knew?"

"Of course, I knew. Why do you think I moved to the other room?"

"Because you didn't want me anymore," she said.

"Oh, lordy, the woman's crazy. Not want you? You're the center of my universe. But you wouldn't talk to me. I didn't know what was going on."

"I thought you married me because you wanted more children. I couldn't let you adopt mine until I was sure I could give you more. Joe, I don't know if I can."

He lifted her until their faces were even. "Anna Crawford, I want you, and Julie and Hank, and any other children we might have. And I grieved over the loss of our baby." Anna's eyes filled with tears and she buried her face against his chest. He lifted her and kissed her gently. "But most of all, I must have you to make my life complete. Remember our wedding night?"

"Oh, yes!" she said fervently.

He laughed. "I said I needed you to be honest, and you agreed."

She ducked her head against his chest. "I got scared and I forgot."

"And now? Tell me what you want."

"I want you, and the kids, and your family, and our

home, but most of all I need you," she said, imitating his earlier statement. "For always."

"And always." He kissed her again.

A knock at the door startled them.

"Yes?" Joe called.

"Daddy, are you and Mommy naked?"

Joe's startled look made Anna laugh. She answered. "No, we're not, sweetie. Come on in."

Julie opened the door, her grandfather standing behind her. Caleb's expression was curious.

"Everything all right?" Caleb asked.

"Everything's wonderful, Dad. Thanks for getting our daughter from school. Tell Mom we communicated and everything's perfect, now." Joe added a big grin to his message even as he let Anna slide down his body until her feet touched the floor.

"Okay, but what's that suitcase for? Are we keeping the kids again?"

"No," Anna said. "The suitcase was a mistake I won't ever make again. Joe loves me."

"Well, of course he does, Anna. We all love you. Well, not like Joe, but like family, you know."

Anna and Joe laughed and Joe assured his father he knew, and now Anna did, too. He was going to adopt the kids and they were a family.

"Does that mean I get a horse?" Julie wanted to know.

"I told you we'd discuss that when Mommy is well, young lady. Right now, she needs to spend more time in bed."

"Aw, Daddy, please?"

"I'm not your grandpa, who you can twist around your finger. I'm your daddy and I have to do what is good for you. Now, come tell us all about school today. Dad, we can move to the kitchen and have some coffee or tea and cookies, if you want."

"That would be good. Your mother has me on a diet."

"Okay. Another good reason for family. To cheat on your diet. Come on, everyone. Let's go to the kitchen."

And he swung Anna into his arms, as if he never intended to let her go. And she didn't protest. It was exactly what she wanted.

Epilogue

The alarm went off and Anna forced herself to pull away from the warm nest of Joe's arms and sit up. Then big hands grabbed her around the waist and pulled her back to him. "Where are you going?

"The alarm went off. If you want breakfast," she pointed out, determination in her voice, "you'd best let me up."

"That's a tough choice," he protested.

"Joe Crawford, you need your breakfast," she said as she pushed away from him and sat up again. Then, with a sudden movement, she covered her mouth with her hands and rushed to the bathroom.

"Anna? What's wrong?" Joe called as he threw back the cover and followed her, worry in his eyes.

Anna felt better after vomiting the remains of her dinner from last night. To Joe's surprise, she was grinning. "I think your next child just announced his or her presence."

"What? Are you sure?"

"No, but I'll get a test at the store today." Her calmness worried him. He picked her up again and carried her back to bed.

"I'll get the test. You'll stay in bed," he ordered.

"Joe, I can't stay in bed for nine months!"

"Maybe not, but you can stay in bed this morning. Can you eat anything?"

"Yes. I'll go back to sleep for a little while. Then I'll be ready for food." She smiled at him again and her happiness got through to him. They were going to have a baby. They'd certainly hoped for one, but Joe had Anna, Julie and Hank. He wasn't going to be greedy.

"You really think you're pregnant?"

She nodded.

"Yahoo!" he whooped, leaning over to kiss her again.

He'd been blessed with the woman he loved. Now they were going to add to their happiness with another child. He couldn't believe his good luck. "I'm going to call everyone right now and—"

"No, Joe, not yet. Let's be sure."

"Okay. But when I buy that test, half the town will know before lunch," he warned.

"But we'll know before they do. Then you can call your parents and the rest of the family. Our baby will only be five months younger than Lindsay's baby. He'll have someone to play with."

"And he'll have the best family in the world," Joe said, kissing her again.

"Yes. He's going to be one lucky baby."

* * * * *

Don't miss Judy Christenberry's
newest release from Silhouette Books.

HUSH

is on sale in September and features more of
the Crawford family as well as a long-hidden
secret that will change all their lives.

If you enjoyed what you just read,
then we've got an offer you can't resist!

Take 2 bestselling love stories FREE!

Plus get a FREE surprise gift!

Clip this page and mail it to Silhouette Reader Service™

IN U.S.A.	**IN CANADA**
3010 Walden Ave.	P.O. Box 609
P.O. Box 1867	Fort Erie, Ontario
Buffalo, N.Y. 14240-1867	L2A 5X3

YES! Please send me 2 free Silhouette Romance® novels and my free surprise gift. After receiving them, if I don't wish to receive anymore, I can return the shipping statement marked cancel. If I don't cancel, I will receive 6 brand-new novels every month, before they're available in stores! In the U.S.A., bill me at the bargain price of $3.34 plus 25¢ shipping and handling per book and applicable sales tax, if any*. In Canada, bill me at the bargain price of $3.80 plus 25¢ shipping and handling per book and applicable taxes**. That's the complete price and a savings of at least 10% off the cover prices—what a great deal! I understand that accepting the 2 free books and gift places me under no obligation ever to buy any books. I can always return a shipment and cancel at any time. Even if I never buy another book from Silhouette, the 2 free books and gift are mine to keep forever.

215 SDN DNUM
315 SDN DNUN

Name	(PLEASE PRINT)	
Address	Apt.#	
City	State/Prov.	Zip/Postal Code

* Terms and prices subject to change without notice. Sales tax applicable in N.Y.
** Canadian residents will be charged applicable provincial taxes and GST.
All orders subject to approval. Offer limited to one per household and not valid to current Silhouette Romance® subscribers.
® are registered trademarks of Harlequin Books S.A., used under license.

SROM02 ©1998 Harlequin Enterprises Limited

eHARLEQUIN.com

For **FREE online reading,** visit
www.eHarlequin.com now and enjoy:

Online Reads
Read **Daily** and **Weekly** chapters from
our Internet-exclusive stories by your
favorite authors.

Red-Hot Reads
Turn up the heat with one of our more
sensual online stories!

Interactive Novels
Cast your vote to help decide how these
stories unfold…then stay tuned!

Quick Reads
For shorter romantic reads, try our
collection of Poems, Toasts, & More!

Online Read Library
Miss one of our online reads?
Come here to catch up!

Reading Groups
Discuss, share and rave with other
community members!

For great reading online,
visit www.eHarlequin.com today!

INTONL

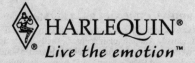

SILHOUETTE *Romance*

COMING NEXT MONTH

#1684 LOVE, YOUR SECRET ADMIRER—Susan Meier
Marrying the Boss's Daughter

Sarah Morris's makeover turned a few heads—including Matt Burke's, her sexy boss! But Matt's life plan didn't include romance. Tongue-tied and jealous, he tried to help Sarah discover her secret admirer's identity, but would he realize *he'd* been secretly admiring her all along?

#1685 WHAT A WOMAN SHOULD KNOW—Cara Colter

Tally Smith wanted a stable home for her orphaned nephew—and that meant marriage. Enter JD Turner, founder of the "Ain't Getting Married, No Way Never Club"—and Jed's biological father. Tally only thought it fair to give the handsome, confirmed bachelor the first shot at being a daddy…!

#1686 TO KISS A SHEIK—Teresa Southwick
Desert Brides

Heart-wounded single father Sheik Fariq Hassan didn't trust beautiful women, so hired nanny Crystal Rawlins disguised her good looks. While caring for his children, she never counted on Fariq's smoldering glances and knee-weakening embraces. But could he forgive her deceit when he saw the real Crystal?

#1687 WHEN LIGHTNING STRIKES TWICE—Debrah Morris
Soulmates

Joe Mitchum was a thorn in Dr. Mallory Peterson's side—then an accident left his body inhabited by her former love's spirit. Unable to tell Mallory the truth, the new Joe set out to change her animosity to adoration. But if he didn't succeed soon their souls would spend eternity apart….

#1688 RANSOM—Diane Pershing

Between a robbery, a ransom and a renegade cousin, Hallie Fitzgerald didn't have time for Marcus Walcott, the good-looking—good-kissing!—overprotective new police chief. So why was he taking a personal interest in her case? Any why was *she* taking such a personal interest in *him*?!

#1689 THE BRIDAL CHRONICLES—Lissa Manley

Jilted once, Ryan Cavanaugh had no use for wealthy women and no faith in love. But the lovely Anna Sinclair seemed exactly as she appeared—a hardworking wedding dress designer. Could their tender bond break through the wall around Ryan's heart…and survive the truth about Anna's secret identity?

SRCNM0803